T0129141

THE PLAYA'S WAY

THE PLAYA'S WAY

CLIFTON HICKEY

THE PLAYA'S WAY

iUniverse books may be ordered through booksellers or by contacting:

iUniverse
1663 Liberty Drive
Bloomington, IN 47403
www.iuniverse.com
1-800-Authors (1-800-288-4677)

ISBN: 978-1-4917-8809-7 (sc)
ISBN: 978-1-4917-8810-3 (e)

Library of Congress Control Number: 2016900780

Print information available on the last page.

iUniverse rev. date: 11/21/2016

PROLOGUE

From the Peach state comes the city slicker, Nard, whose capabilities to captivate the precious mind of a dime is IMPECCABLE! In fact, too flawless until he decides to intervene in a couples most sacred vows: 'TIL DEATH...DO US PART'!

On the other side of things, Shontae, a past, present, and future affiliate of Nard, makes his playa' demeanor say NO to late night rendezvouses and YES to romancing her however she sees fit. Once all said and done, to avoid losing his life and stripes, Nard must listen to his corner and watch for the hook...

CHAPTER: 1

As the early morning dew is greeted by rushing traffic from kids making their en route towards a familiar place, some seem to be a bit sluggish while others chant on in approval the finally awaited first day of school. The year is 1998 and from the looks of things, "GOOD MORNING AMERICA!" Freddy Junior High School, home of the Blue Devils, entrance doors were packed with continuous movement trying desperately to flood the hallways. Greetings of all sorts were in full effect: Teachers with teachers, teachers and students, students with familiar identity of those well known to some never seen before. School pranks usually consist of toilet paper thrown across the trees but this years joke displayed paint smeared over the faculty parking lot in huge letters, which reads: "SCHOOL SUCKS! LET'S ALL DUCK!" The principal wasted no time announcing his disgust over the intercom and of permanent termination caused to the damaged property once the student was apprehended.

Shouting voices and slamming lockers extended the ongoing gathering. Her dominant persona sashayed itself quietly from around the corner, freezing every boy's movement who acknowledged her beauty strut past. Silence had managed to overtake the hallway ruckus. Drooling mouths began staining the tile floor. Girls who watched on displayed a sign of dissatisfaction by turning their noses up and eyelids down. She shared brief greetings with a chosen few, due to the majority disliking her demeanor upon approaching her assigned locker.

Bernard studied her every movement under a watchful eye. She came to a stop at a locker and placed some books inside. He decided to creep from behind unnoticed. The locker door partially begun to close before noticing him leaning against a locker next to hers.

"Hi! Remember me?"

"How could I forget?! As many times I've told you NO to being my boyfriend last year, I'm surprised to see you still making a fool out of yourself."

He approached closer, observing her entire attire from top to bottom, making sure no flaws were noticeable.

"What do you think you're doing?"

"What's it look like I'm doing? I'm checkin' you out."

"Haven't you caught on—"She stepped away from her locker and was followed, "—you're not my type."

He extended a hand, which grazed the curled tips of the hair resting at the base of her shoulders.

"BOY!" She attempted a swift blockage. "WHAT'S WRONG WITH YOU?"

"Chill out, girl! Damn! Can't a youngin' double check yo' parents' work?"

She eyed him in disgust, commenting, "Child, please."

Her constant denial in being a part of his life in the past made the thrill of the chase that much more interesting to him. He figured today would clearly establish his message that this school year would be no different from last year in that he'd try to make her his girlfriend.

She eventually entered her class. He paused outside the door, contemplating if he should continue on with his mission or allow her to escape another day. A vacant desk stationed behind her seemed the perfect reason to further pursue his dream.

"Good morning, class," announced the teacher, "and welcome back to another WONDERFUL school year." She scribbled her name across the chalkboard. "My name is Ms. Stewart and I will be your home economics teacher for this entire school semester."

His desk clacked lightly across the floor, moving closer towards hers. She quickly grew agitated upon witnessing him seated behind her.

"I'm sayin', baby, why you makin' this so hard for the both of us?"

She whispered in return, "It's only hard because you're hard-headed."

"Maybe because you actin' like you don't want me when deep down inside, I know you do."

"You know what, you're absolutely right. I do want you. I want you to—" she turned her face sharply towards his and blurted, "LEAVE ME ALONE!"

Loud laughter erupted throughout the classroom before the students silenced themselves. The teacher stood motionless in front of the chalkboard. Everyone focused their attention on him. He slowly began to sink downward in his seat.

"YOUNG MAN!" yelled Ms. Stewart.

He appeared dumbfounded by her outburst. "Who, ME?"

"Yes, YOU! You're the only young man in this classroom with all girls. Can you please tell me why is that?"

"In fact," he said as he regained his composure, "I think I can, Ms. Stewart." He gazed into the inquiring eyes of the surrounding students. "Cause judging by the looks of things, I'd have to say that the rest of the young men would rather chase snakes, snails and puppy dog tails."

The girl in front of him struggled to hold in her laugh. He felt pleased knowing their morning togetherness wasn't a complete waste of time. Ms. Stewart totally disagreed, finding his response inexcusable.

"Well, sir, how about you chase the hallway to the principal's office? NOW!"

She pointed at the door for him to hurriedly depart her class. He slowly lifted himself up out of the seat, but not before signaling to the girl to call him later on.

The principal rocked back and forth at his desk, already aware of Bernard's class disturbance. He watched him pull open the office door. He sat at his usual location in the corner, locking his sight in on the principal. A finger rested up against his temple, signaling a sign of uncertainty regarding what punishment to apply or whether to inform his parents. Deciding with his second choice, he grabbed ahold of the phone. The conversation led to a brief explanation pertaining to the scenario and of their needed assistance at school immediately.

It seemed as if it were only yesterday, having entered through that same door discussing the same problem with his parents and the principal. His eyes wondered around the walls, filled with certificates and photos. The slightest sound heard outside the office door forced his head to flinch in its direction. As it all started to unfold, the principal, along with his parents, were escorted inside.

"Please have a seat, Mr. and Mrs. Hick," he said, signaling at a bench beside their son.

"What seems to be the problem, sir?" asked Mr. Hick.

"Well," he said, clearing his throat, "your son continues, as the year before, to bother our students again during class."

"Boy, is that right?" Bernard nodded in agreement, and questioned the principal. "And what's wrong with that?"

Mrs. Hick's dismay directed itself at her husband.

"For one, he's here to receive an education and two, he is also keeping his classmates from doing their work."

"I agree with you one hundred percent, sir," stated Mrs. Hick. "Which is why I will be dealing with my son PERSONALLY when he gets home."

She exchanged a hardened look with him.

"For what?" spoke Mr. Hick authoritatively. "All because he finds some young girl attractive? At least he does have something positive on his mind instead of trying to hang out with bad boys while vandalizing school property."

Mr. Hick rubbed a hand over his son's head. He sat in silence, enjoying the way his dad was handling the situation.

"He's still a kid, sir, and there will be plenty of time for all that. But for right now, at this very moment, I'm trying to run a decent school with as little of the disturbance as possible."

Mr. Hick stood to his feet and approached the principal's desk.

"I tell you what, MR. PRINCIPAL," he said, leaning inward while placing his palms flat on the desktop. "Would you prefer for your son to learn at an early age about the opposite sex, or when it's too late and catch him in the act with some boy sticking his—"

"CARL!"

Mrs. Hick interrupted her husband's remaining remarks, knowing the damage his anger would cause. He stepped away from the desk and angled his movement towards the direction in which he entered.

"Honey, when you finish, I'm outside this door. Come on, son."

Bernard sprung out of the seat, bypassing his father in a hurry, who slammed the door behind them.

"I'm sorry, sir, but it's just that…sometimes, my husband gets very uptight with those in disagreement about our son liking girls so much."

"I understand that, Mrs. Hick. All I was trying to do was let him know that this is a place for an education. Not about how a boy flirts with a girl."

The two stationed themselves on a couple of chairs some few yards down outside the principal's office. His son's behavior reminded him of himself when he acted out in a similar way, or sometimes even worse during his school years. The minor harm his son caused bothered him none, but to deny himself a free education by wasting valuable time scored a zero in his gradebook.

"But the girl was pretty, Dad!"

"I believe you, son, but you must do those types of things on your own time. Your dad used to do the same thing too when I was your age. Hell, even now and then I get a lil' careless, but don't tell yo' mother." He shared a smile. "What I'm sayin', son, is catch her in the hallway and not during class cause I'd prefer for you to get an education first, then chase girls later on."

"You know I will. I always do. And plus, this is the first day of school and all I was tryin' to do was have a lil' fun."

He slid his arm around his son's neck, stating, "Too much horseplayin' and not enough work will only leave you broke, lonely, and hurt. Is that what you want out of life?" His son's head slowly signaled "no". Mrs. Hick walked out of the office and spotted them to her left. She headed in their direction. "Well, continue to make your dad proud, alright?"

"The principal said he's only going to give you this one warning," intervened Mrs. Hick. "The next time, it's suspension."

"Yes, ma'am. I'm sorry, momma."

"You should be, cause I am not going to keep going through this mess with you year in and year out."

"Take it easy, honey. The boy gets the picture."

"And as for you, Mr. Hick, we have some unfinished business to attend to because your behavior back there was uncalled for."

He slid up to his wife, planting a swift kiss across her lips. "Yes, ma'am. I'm sorry too, momma." He smothered her in his arms.

"Well, I betta' gone and get to class. The girls are waiting on me." He cautiously stepped away from his parents after acknowledging his mother's disapproval of the word "girl". "Just kiddin'. See y'all two later." He made a run for it down the hallway.

CHAPTER: 2

Bernard's first day of school ended on its usual troubled start. Ducking verbal assault by scolding staff didn't cease until his feet were safely off school property. Compared to last year's write-ups and extra duties, he escaped unharmed, but with numerous warnings. His walk home was several blocks away, and he soon neared it. The closer he approached, the more his ears picked up on the loud music— probably due to Belinda, his high school babysitter, awaiting his arrival. To no surprise, she lingered in the center floor of the living room, dancing to the blaring sounds. She removed his school books from within his hands and tossed them on the couch in need of a dance partner.

"What's wrong with you, woman?"

"I'm gettin' my freak on. Why? Is that a problem?"

"Nope!"

She had always appeared to him, over the past, as an attractive young lady—someone with a voluptuous figure, but in all the right places. She squeezed him tighter, finding their embracement humorous. His head rested gently against her plump breasts. Deciding to take further action into his own hands, he swung her around, gripping her by the waist, and grinded his body up against her buttocks.

"What in the world are you doing, sir?" she asked, coming to a standstill.

"I'm 'bout to turn you out, if that's okay with you."

She considered his request, found it quite amusing, and gave in to his demands. He started to slap her across the derriere repeatedly until she decided enough was enough. She left him standing alone, headed in the direction of the radio, lowering the volume.

"I'm too much for you, I suppose."

"Nah, not really. It was best we stopped while you still had a chance."

"They tell me 'don't start it if you can't finish it'."

She strolled to the couch and took a seat. He mimicked her actions, placing his body down beside her.

"Oh, believe me, if you wasn't such a baby, I would've been turned you out a long time ago."

"That makes two, baby girl."

"Where did you get such a slick mouth?"

"Like father, like son. It's a gift already in me."

"You're right about that, cause yo' pop's hands do get a lil' careless from time to time."

"Can we help it that you was born with such cute features?"

His compliment came as a surprise, forcing a reddish shade to coat her yellow complexion.

"You're kinda' cute yo' damn self."

She pinched him on the cheek.

"Cut it out with the foolishness, woman," he said, rubbing the spot she squeezed. "Do you realize what you've done? Now my face might be all bruised up. If you want me for yourself, at least be a lot more gentle with the prized possession."

"Boy, please," she said, sliding off the couch.

"Hold on, young lady. Where do you think you're goin'? I ain't done with you yet."

"To the bathroom. Why? You wanna come?"

"Hell yeah!"

Making her way inside, she turned around to notice his distance just a couple steps away from invading her privacy. She closed the door on him in the nick of time.

"SIIIIIIKE," she yelled from inside the bathroom.

He stood on the outside, fumbling with the door handle, hoping to find it unlocked. His body laid resting up against it, pleading in desperation for her to possibly allow him entrance.

"Come on, Belinda! I won't tell if you don't!"

"You're too young," she blurted.

"You're too old to be actin' like I'm too young!"

A flushing sound halted their ongoing dialogue momentarily. The door eventually opened. He stepped back while she stood in the doorway.

"What could you possibly do with all of this?" She made an outer motion of her vagina with her hands.

"Smack it. Flip it. Then stroke it down."

Her attempt at a swift move past him went unsuccessful. He caught ahold of her wrist, placing her arm around his neck. He stationed an arm around the base of her waist.

"Boy, you probably don't even know where to put it, do you?"

He continued guiding her direction around through the house with his hand lowered over her booty.

"Woman, just follow my lead," he assured her.

The door to his bedroom rested partly ajar. He used his foot to widen its entrance. A couple posters of male rap artists along with a majority of female R&B celebrities covered most of his bedroom wall. His bed frame was designed in the form of an early 70's model Cadillac with gold trimmings. The blanket covering his bed displayed dices and diamonds on it. He sat her down at the foot of the bed, wasting no time in extending his lips before being embraced back by hers.

Her mouth separated from his mentioning, "And by the way... PLEASE be sure to be gentle."

A brief giggle followed her own remark. Up to now, he had shown complete confidence in his actions. His bodily demeanor began displaying a slight sign of timidness. She sat up, wondering why undressing himself took so long after hearing about his acquired skills in mingling with the opposite sex. She knew the signs of fear he displayed all too well, and figured the best way to settle his nerves was by partaking in his troubles. The zipper to his pants, which kept him preoccupied, easily slid down at the control of her fingers. She laid back on the bed, sliding her lower attire off from around her waist and ankles. Her legs spread apart. The weight of his body eventually rested itself against hers.

"Now where does it go?" he inquired.

Her loud laughter startled him.

"As smart as your mouth is, I would've at least thought you would have known where to put it. Give me a few seconds. My baby is dry anyway."

Her fingers glided across her pubic hair, making their way in the direction of her opening flesh. After a brief moment of self-indulgence, she grabbed him by his erection, sliding it within her.

"At least you do have a lil' something I can work with," she commented. "Now, slow and easy, start to move in an in-and-out motion. Slow now."

"You mean like this?"

His body gradually began to stroke in a frail manner.

"Mmm-hmm," she said, expressing her eroticism. "Just like that."

Time elapsed some forty to forty-five minutes. He cleaned himself up and walked around throughout the house in his underwear while smoking a cigarette. Belinda left shortly ago. His parents were due in at any moment. He reclined out on the living room couch, viewing T.V. The sound of slamming car doors outside the window disturbed his peace. Identifying his parents through the curtains, he sprint to the bathroom, flushing the cigarette down the toilet. A can of Lysol spray off the bathroom shelf was used to try and diffuse the smoke. He tossed the can into his bedroom and repositioned himself back on the couch, bracing for his parents' entrance.

"What up, momma?"

"Hay, boy." She lifted her nose, trying to distinguish the odor detected in the air. "What in the world is that I smell?"

"Smells like smoke," stated Mr. Hick, who continued to walk on through the living room.

"I know damn well you ain't been smoking in my house, boy. In fact, I know damn well you ain't been smoking, period."

"No, ma'am," he said, staring at her convincingly. "Belinda's ride came inside with a cigarette in his mouth."

"That girl knows that's a house rule on the 'don't do' list while she's in here. I'm going to have to talk with her when she comes back over again." She kicked off her shoes and reclined out on the couch, trying to massage the pain in her foot. "And what are you doing with nothing but some underwear on yo' butt while sitting on my couch? Boy, you done bumped yo' head! Go put some clothes on before you have help losing the ones you got on now."

"Noooooo problem, momma."

He hopped off the couch, heading to his bedroom. Shortly after entering, his father walked in with both hands tucked down in his pants pockets.

"You aiight, son?"

"Yeah, dad. What makes you say that?"

"I don't know. You tell me. Maybe you can update me on a few things. I mean, you walkin' around in your underwears. Out there sitting on your mother's couch, half naked. Something ain't right cause that's definitely not like you." He avoided eye contact with his father while continuing to dress. "What you should've done was sprayed in here and changed them bedsheets cause the odor of some female is very displeasing."

He stepped further inside the room and shut the door. Bernard stood motionless. His fathered lingered directly over him, waiting for him to look up. His head inched itself upward at a snail's pace.

"DAD! I CAN EX—"

"Son, the only explaining I need to hear is did you enjoy it and was it the babysitter?"

He hesitated a moment before responding. "Yes...and yes."

"Got to be more careful! Better you than me, son, because she'll still be laid out begging for an early release. Gone and do something with that odor on your bed before your mother gets hot on your trail."

"Yes, sir."

He watched him turn to walk out, but stopped short of a complete departure.

"'Too-Smooth Nard'! How does that nickname fit you?"

"I like it, Dad. Short for Bernard."

"Oh, and by the way, I'll give you several pieces of advice to live by and never leave home without them. The first one is always, ALWAYS use a condom. If you didn't, we'll go to a clinic as soon as possible to make sure she didn't pass anything over to you. And secondly, the most important one of them all…the next time you have her pent down or any other woman, never let up until she gives up."

He winked an eye at his son before departing the room. Nard went over to his bed to take a whiff of the cover and frowned up in disgust.

CHAPTER: 3

Growing up as youth, the question children are asked is: "What do you want to be when you grow up?" The usual response to such a question is a fireman, a lawyer, a doctor, or even the President. Traveling through life, a person's dreams preoccupy most of the childhood minds, which further instill inspiration to try and achieve goals attainable. After maturing to adult status, when asked are they anywhere close to who they stated as a child, the majority will respond: "NO!" Nine times out of ten, the picture painted in front of you is of what you were only allowed to be, meaning it's not easy to answer a question without the full concept of the question itself. You be what you can! Nothing more, nothing less.

Though, who would've figured that Nard's latter life, due to his childhood altercations with girls, would lay the foundation for being a womanizer of any choice he so chooses. Practice makes perfect. Mistakes bring cautiousness. And during his high school years, with his unsuccessful tries, came a million and one minor mistakes: too much up and close, leaving her little breathing room, or ignoring her to the point where she ignores him altogether. Every once in a while, he would hit the bull's eye and play his position to a perfect tune, very similar to a Rick James and Tina Marie classic, "Fire and Desire". But then again, with time comes a reality, bringing into existence a better way of strategizing his steps to a more successful meaning.

Strolling around Peachtree Mall on an early Saturday morning, Nard purchased a couple of items from several different men's clothing stores. Dazzled by her entrance into the mall on his way out, it brought their distant "hellos" face to face. A beauty mark rested just above her corner lip. Her light, greenish eyes were enlivened by the sunrays that beamed through the glass roof. He whispered some words in her ear, which forced her to laugh. She stood in awe, unable to focus her undivided attention but on him only.

"Damn! We just met and you're already makin' it hard for a brotha' to leave you."

"Don't. Come stroll with me for a while through the mall and I promise you I'll make your stay worth it," she said, pulling at his hand.

"I tell you what," he said, shortening the space between their stance, "how 'bout I leave you with this?" His lips gently grazed her darkened cheek. "And I promise you the next time our togetherness won't be so short, along with the kiss as well."

"I'll be waiting, big boy."

She allowed his hand to escape her grasp. He looked on as she turned and walked away, hypnotizing his mind with her seductive stride that had been well-rehearsed for many occasions such as this one. The trance he was in eventually subsided, and he turned to exit the mall. The sun's brightness forced him to lower the Atlanta Braves ball cap he wore, which shielded the sight of his pupils almost completely. He lifted his head about an inch upward in search of his car. Through his close surveillance stood beauty fumbling with a set of keys four to five car-lengths over in the next lane. Her thickness in plain denim shorts and a pink tank top deterred his direction, and he analyzed her every movement in an effort to catch up before she departed.

"Hol—hol—hold up, miss."

"Excuse me?"

She seemed agitated by his disturbance. His sudden closeness had him within reaching distance. A peculiar look of familiarity unraveled through his sight as he couldn't believe what he was seeing, or was about to say.

"Shontae!" He expressed excitement. "Remember me?!"

He removed his cap. Her thoughts boggled over his identity before she showed a sign of gloating. She extended her face up to his, making sure the individual was not deceiving her and focused in on his last two words spoken.

"NARD! From junior high school!"

She confirmed herself in a tone of astonishment as he politely accepted it.

"Pretty much."

"Man! I can't believe it's you! Look at you! Full beard. Cornrows. Honey brown complexion. Great shape."

"Six-foot, two-inch and one hundred and ninety-five pound frame to be exact."

"I see time had done you much good since the last time we met."

"You know, a lil' touch-up here and there from the barbershop can work wonders for us all."

They embraced each other for a short span.

"So, how you been makin' it, Shontae?"

"I can't complain, and, from the looks of it," she glanced over his posture, "you can't either. What's been up with you?"

"Same ol', same ol'. 'Bout ready to cover tracks from way back."

"Oh, really?"

Leaning beside her ride, he asked, "You don't mind if we converse for a minute, do you? That is, if I ain't holding you up."

"I see some things haven't changed about you."

"For you, cutie, all the time. A brotha' can still remember that first day of school massacre I received with you yelling at me."

She stood between her driver's door and rested one foot on the floorboard. Her purse flopped onto the passenger seat from her toss.

"You act like you couldn't take no for an answer. What else was I going to do?"

"Cop a plea until further notice from me."

"Please! And I suppose we are right back where we left off then too."

"How do you want it? At least I get this opportunity to let an 'associate' know that ain't no love lost at all."

"Is it too late for an apology?"

"That depends. Let's see..." He studied his fingers, weighing the good and bad that manifested between them in the past. "An apology is aiight, but you sort of made school difficult for me, being that you never gave a brotha' the time of day and whatnot."

"How 'bout this. An apology and my number."

"Hold up," he said, raising himself off the front side of the car. "Did I hear what I thought I just heard or are my ears deceiving me?"

He leaned his head inward, close to hers.

"No, silly. I'm willing to let bygones be bygones. That is, if you feel the same way."

"It's your call. You been being able to make a big girl decision. Handle yo' business."

She sat down on her front seat, scuffling for a piece of paper out of the glove compartment.

"And by the way," he said, resting his hand on her door, "you still look good too."

She handed him the piece of paper.

"You too. Now that you're much older."

"I ain't mad at'cha. But you hold it down until otherwise aiight."

"You do the same. Bye, Bernard."

He stepped back and shut her door. Her hand extended outward, waving him goodbye.

CHAPTER: 4

The morning hours had exceeded towards mid-noon. Nard's direction led him to Grandma Jarrett's front lawn, twenty minutes outside Columbus city limits. Her neighborhood resembled the sight of a prehistoric landmark. Spacious yards were evenly squared off by white picket fences. Front porches designed off a wooden-stair banister. A two-lane road stretched for over several miles with a speed limit of fifteen through the heart of her small town. Just before departing the county line sat a fire station and one antique firetruck. Stationed across the street rested the town sheriff, comfortably in his rocking chair on post.

In the past, she insisted on her late husband finding a more suitable location to call home instead of surrounded themselves with predominately all-white counterparts during the early 1960s. Grandpa Jarrett lost his life at the hands of his racist environment after leaving a tavern late one night with Mrs. Jarrett alongside. Three Caucasians rode by, tossing a bottle, coming within inches of Mrs. Jarrett's face. The car tires came to a halt before Mr. Jarrett could finish shouting his anger. They drove in reverse up beside them. A man exited the back seat, staggering to his feet. His friends cackled and promoted his ignorance on in any way imaginable.

"Woul—would you...BOY, ru—run that," he said, wiping his mouth dry from saliva dripped down the side, "by yo' massa' ears one mo' t-time, nigga?"

Mrs. Jarrett begged of her husband to overlook the man and simply walk away. His stubbornness wouldn't allow him to retreat.

His father taught him as a child to defend for himself against the racist American society under any circumstances. Mr. Jarrett stared the pale-faced man deeply in his drunken eyes.

"What I said, BOY, is to quit acting like cowards and be real men like this real negro."

A bottle slid out of the drunkard's hand, shattering on the sidewalk. Mr. Jarrett's words had numbed the man's body completely. The commotion inside the car froze to a silence. The outside air grew still. He watched his adversaries under close surveillance for any sign of sudden movement.

"Sss-sir," he said, breaking the tense silence, "uuu-you mmm-might be right. Weee didn't ma-mean no harm, sir. Sssssssorry 'bout that, ma'aaam."

Mrs. Jarrett felt satisfied with the man's apology. He bowed his head, excusing them to walk past him. She quickly grabbed her husband's hand, bypassing him in a hurry. The stranger swiftly bent downward for a long portion of broken glass at the bottle's throat and forced its jagged edge into the slinder neck of Mr. Jarrett. Blood squirted profusely from the wound. His body tumbled helplessly to the ground. Mrs. Jarrett fell to her knees in screams beside him. Taillights were last seen of the suspect's getaway, to never be tried in the court of law.

On the night of the incident, the town went into an outrage for up to twenty-four hours. The tavern they hung out at together that night had been set aflame by a rowdy crowd of African Americans, where whites mainly gathered. The National Guard was summoned to place the rioters under control. After the death of Mr. Jarrett, she vowed to live out her remaining life in the house he purchased, raising their eight kids, even if it meant dying by the ignorance of her surrounding peers.

Since then, her day-to-day chores around the house kept her grounded and peaceful. Her gray and white fluffy housecat traveled at her heels any time she made a move. Nard made it his duty in seeing to it that his grandmother was taken good care of for as long as he'd been driving. He approached her screen door, yelling, "Honey,

I'm home!" Grandma Jarrett stepped out of the kitchen and into her living room. She wiped her wet hands dry on an apron tied around her waist. The housecat circled his ankles.

"Hay, son."

"Hay, grandma."

He gave her a hug and kiss on the cheek.

"What brings you to this side of town? What done happened? One of them gals you been messin' with done gave you some bad news and you need some ol' grandma advice?"

"Nah, Grandma. Ain't nuthin' like that. You know your favorite grandson had to stop by and make sure his two beautiful ladies were doing better than the day before."

"God bless you, child, cause I do need for you to run and pick up a few items from the store for me and Miss Lady Fur."

"Put it down on paper and leave the rest up to me."

He faced the large portrait of his grandfather located on the piano and saluted him as he normally did. The many great stories told when he was a child about how Grandpa Jarrett struggled hard to be respected in a segregated society influenced him to live a more obedient lifestyle of his own. Today's racism still existed, but in a hidden format: CORPORATE CORRECTIONS OF AMERICA, Inc.! Nard had several friends that were gang-affiliated growing up in the neighborhood which led to trouble. After run-ins with the law pertaining to petty offenses, he soon realized the importance of an education and placed his head deeper into schoolbooks.

"Here you go, son," she said, handing him the paper wrapped around some money. "I sho' do appreciate it."

"Now, you know it wouldn't be right if I didn't see to everything being aiight with you, Grandma. I'm just mad you don't call me more often for my help."

"Thank you for the reassurance, son, and I will be taking you up on that offer."

"Be back shortly with everything."

He kissed her once more on the cheek before leaving.

"Take your time, son," she yelled through the screen door.

The items he viewed on the list exceeded her normal purchase at the gas station not too far around the corner. He would drive to a convenience store in his city that supplied the extra items she requested on paper. To him, there were no limits when it came time for taking care of his grandmother or any other relative of such. Blood was always thicker than water and he promised himself to instill the same importance in his own future kids.

He cautiously spied Slim, his stepbrother, inside the store standing over a variety of potato chips down an aisle. In stealth mode he maneuvered low and unseen, hoping to surprise him. The sound of his ringtone was a dead giveaway, alerting Slim of his presence.

"I'm sayin, what you doin' all out of bounds on this side of thangs?"

"You know how shit be. One of my shawtys' needed a brotha for support. Back support. She said she was experiencing some early morning side effects makin it hard to stop touchin herself.

"I can feel you on that."

"Being the equipped fixer that I am, all leaks are sealed, you dig. By the way, I know you heard the spot supposed to be hot for the night, right?"

"Nah. What's up? Update a playa'."

"Dime Dimensions!"

"You mean, if her ass ain't fine, no inside."

"Anythang under a 9.9 definitely can't slide inside."

"Well, catch me doing me and then some at the bar posted up."

"But kenfolks, let me pay fo' this and get back to the barbershop cause me and my dividends definitely actin' like we ain't ken'."

"No doubt. Oh, and before I make my presence felt at double D's tonight, I plan on stopping by the shop to see what's happenin' with everyone else."

"Get at us folks."

"Peace."

Grandma met him on her porch on his way back in. He placed the money she gave him for the goods along with extras in the grocery bag earlier, knowing she would refuse any of his donations offered as help. She could have thrown it away as far as he was concerned but he would be long gone before she had any chance of protesting his kindness.

The pollen-covered convertible Benz he drove influenced him enough for an afternoon of cleaning. He kept the utensils needed at his mother's home, where he temporarily resided. His place of residence was under remodeling until further notice. The unexpected encounters he had to endure with her forced him to stay on high alert for her whereabouts while inside. Her lectures and physical abuse sometimes belittled his character. He wondered if she would one day view him as an adult and not just a mother's child. He decided early on to move as quickly as possible, undetected, hoping to evade her scanners.

He exited his car, leaving the door ajar, and walked quietly up to the house. The side door he checked was unlocked. His thought of making it in and out safely felt relieving.

Nowhere inside could he detect her presence. For once, he claimed victory. He reached for a cold beer in the refrigerator on his way out, celebrating the moment.

"BOY," she said, tightly grasping ahold of his ear, "why didn't you set out that damn trash this morning before you got up and left headed nowhere?"

He made an attempt at freeing his earlobe.

"Ouch, woman! That hurts!"

"No shit, Sherlock." She released it.

"Ahh-damn, I mean," he said, covering his mouth, "excuse me for my profanity and please accept my apology for forgetting the trash. I tell you what, I'll take it to the nearest dumpster, aiight. You see, problem solved."

"Problem solved, my ass! If you would remember these things like you suppose to, you wouldn't be here in front of me trying to cover those easy-to-notice-ass tracks of yours."

She marveled at her three sons' efforts to evade life's problems using their childhood home for a place of refuge. In return, her strict demands were to have the guestroom organized at dawn, the kitchen in the same exact order the way they found it, and the trash taken out on an early morning departure. No excuses tolerated, or face eviction.

"I'm sorry, momma."

"Yes you are. Sorry. Simple. And some shit. Now make it up to your momma by giving me some money to buy a new dress so your mother can look pretty tonight."

"Where in the hel—, oops," he said, catching his profanity a second time. "Where do you think you're going tonight, woman?"

He dug in his pocket, handing her a thin stack of twenty-dollar bills.

"Oops, none of your damn business. Thank you." She headed to her bedroom, yelling, "AND DON'T FORGET THE TRASH, SON!" He mimicked her underneath his breath. "SAY WHAT, BOY?"

"I SAID AIIGHT," he shouted in return. "Man, this woman don't miss a beat."

He waited for her door to close before tip-toeing to the guestroom. Inside the closet sat a box labeled "Swisher Sweet Finest". He grabbed it off the top shelf. He removed a cigar and slit it down the middle, dumping its contents into a trashcan. A bag of marijuana the size of his thumb was crumbled across the torn leaf. His tongue moistened one side. Rolling the opposite end over into the moist part, he sealed it tight. The huge smile on his face signified finished perfection.

He grabbed ahold of the trash and threw it in his trunk. The pain in his ear reminded him too often of her tough love that would probably continue throughout his remaining life. He laughed at the thought of accepting her abuse, then drove up the block. His GPS displayed several roads left to travel en route to Mike's location. The two shared certain similarities in their demeanors, which made them a force to be reckoned with. Mike stood four inches shorter. A darker complexion. Natural, stocky-built structure described his physique. Wavy hair circled his small cranium. His laziness caused him to lag at unfortunate times, but his certified accountant qualifications guaranteed him an eighty thousand dollar yearly salary.

Nard hadn't informed him of showing up at his doorstep. Compared to Mike's usual delays, any procrastination on his part this afternoon would be exceptional.

"Buuuuuuuu-buuuuuuump!"

Mike stepped out of the front door, seeming a bit sluggish. He wiped a hand across his face, trying to identify the car. A finger signaled Nard to wait while he freshened himself up. His absence reappeared, hopping over the passenger door and into the front seat.

"What up, my nigg?"

"Chillin'. 'Bout to put my foot between your lips if you ever make that leap again."

"No harm intended, sir. Just a lil' excited about getting out of hell's den for a minute. But besides my foolishness, what else is up, up, and away?"

"Our minds. As soon as you place some fire to the tip of this blunt."

"Dearly beloved," preached Mike, taking ahold of the blunt, "what my homeboy have introduced me with today, let no man or woman separate the two of us. Fire from fire," he flicked aflame the lighter he pulled out of his pocket, "blunt to lighter."

"Amen," laughed Nard.

Mike took a long pull off the blunt and started coughing. He lowered the seat further back and passed the blunt over to Nard.

"How we ride tonight, pimpy? No hoes, or many?" questioned Mike.

Nard tried speaking, but gagged from the smoke he withheld in his lungs.

"Wooo! Man," he exclaimed, wiping his watery eyes. "Boy, let me tell you! I guess we ride however time may fly. They say that double D's supposed to have the block on lock so you know what that means."

They faced each other, stating, "GRIND TIME FOR THE FLY GUYS!"

CHAPTER: 5

"Damn, girl! Do you see what just pulled up in the parking lot looking scrumptious and delicious?" Na-Na uttered aloud.

Carmen stood, confused, on rather she referred to the car that turned into the parking lot of Southside Carwash or the two men inside. Na-Na eventually answered Carmen's question, viewing her wave as they drove by.

"Mm, mm, mm," responded Carmen. "Now I know what the rapper Trina meant when she said 'woop-woop, pull over, that ass is too fine'."

Felicia paused from vacuuming her car, commenting, "Both you hoes need to get a grip of yourselves and put those coochies back in the freezer before the heat melt they asses."

"Well, well, well, miss 'my-twat-is-not-the-spot-for-the-lollipop-to-enter'," enlightened Carmen.

"Nooooo-dooooooubt," applauded Na-Na.

Felicia continued cleaning without further sarcasm. She flipped a coin earlier, losing out on the choice of her troublesome friends to tag along. Besides day-to-day living in Bakervillage Apartments, Na-Na and Carmen rarely experienced anything other than their hostile environment. The burden of raising kids without their fathers kept them mostly confined within the tenements' surrounding gates, working to make ends meet. Felicia accepted her title as godmother years ago, making sure the kids were spoiled with gifts every time she paid them a visit.

The strict guidance which sheltered Felicia at home involving both her parents kept her on a decent path towards independency. She earned a degree in business management, later becoming an employee at Google in the financial department. Her two-bedroom condominium overlooked the downtown city lights of Muscogee County. Beauty was another one of her assets, as she once took first place in a county-wide swimsuit competition shortly after graduating from high school. Felicia's friends weren't as attractive as she was, but were well-rounded enough that they gained enough attention whenever they hung out in public.

"So you ladies won't mind me getting first ups in conversing with the owner of that ride?" inquired Felicia. "You know, a lil' brief introduction."

"Sure," said Na-Na.

"Go right ahead," stated Carmen.

Responding together, they said "NO PROBLEM!"

"Oh, and by the way," mentioned Na-Na, "make sure you at least thaw out that ice-age vagina of yours before you do some things that I wouldn't do while it is on deep-freeze."

They all walked over to the parked car. Nard and Mike exited the front seats, viewing the company approach.

"Ladies, ladies, ladies and I do mean ladies. How are we feeling today?" asked Nard.

"Quite arie," informed Carmen in a Jamaican lingo.

"Can we get some kind of greeting going," continued Nard, "cause a brotha' is very skeptical about talking to strangers. Especially three fine-ass strangers."

"I'm Carmen," she said, pointing to the others, "this here is Na-Na and of course, the mentor of the group…Miss Felicia."

"They call me Nard and this is my partna', Mike."

Carmen disrupted their togetherness, spotting Na-Na's baby father lingering at the lower end of the carwash.

"We got company."

Felicia and Na-Na's eyes followed the direction Carmen's face angled. Na-Na squinted in on the male figure reclining in on the passenger seat of someone's car.

"What in the hell does he want?" mentioned Na-Na, appearing somewhat annoyed. "Excuse me, everyone, but there seems to be a dog who's broken his leash and sniffed me out."

"With the odor you tote between yo' legs, that definitely shouldn't have been hard for him to do," teased Carmen.

Na-Na walked off, but not without raising her middle finger at her friends.

"But as we were before we was so rudely interrupted," spoke Felicia, standing closer to Nard.

"Give the brotha' a lil' breathing room, Felicia. Damn!"

"Woman, you can mind or find you some business of your own and let mines handle mines."

"Anyway," she said, displaying the flat side of her palm towards Felicia's face, insistant an immediate cease of her gibberish.

"Damn, shawty. I see you and yo' homegirls carry it like some ol' Lavern and Shirly type of drama," Nard said to Felicia.

"All the time. Them my dogs. We have a tendency of letting it be known wherever, around whoever." She slightly moved her face inward up to his. "Nard, why your eyelids so low? You been smoking that stuff?"

He expressed a grin, somewhat amused by the curiosity in her voice.

"You can't tell! Listen to how slow they speech is," informed Carmen.

"I'm sayin', would you prefer to see a brotha' at the corner of some street with a sign in his hand that reads 'WILL WASH YO' ASS FOR CRACK'?" spoke Mike.

"Boy, you are craaaaazy," said Carmen.

"You think that's crazy, young lady. How 'bout coming a lil' closer so I can whisper one in your ear real quick that's waaay too explicit for our minor friends we're with."

He signaled for her to move within whispering distance.

"You don't smoke every day, do you, Nard?" questioned Felicia. "I mean, you do have a normal life to attend to, don't you?"

"Of course not, baby girl. Mostly on weekend rendezvouses while running across pretty chicks, such as yourself, do I usually allow my mind to be a bit abnormal and analyze the more funnier part of a person's natural traits. You know, viewing them for who they really are."

"Forcing them to smoke too, probably."

"It ain't even like that with me."

"Well, exactly how is it, then?"

"Shiiit, you know, everything in stride."

"I bet."

She stood in front of him, holding a suspicious look on her face.

"One thing for certain," he said, rubbing his stomach, "it does give a brotha' the munchies cause my belly is being tight squeezed by nothin'." He scanned the entire parking lot, spotting the car she was cleaning. "Which one of you ladies own that ride y'all are in?"

"It's mine, sexy," verified Felicia.

"Is that right?" A share of flirtatious stares had their eyes glued to one another. "Then, would it be a problem if we sent yo' friend and mines on they merry way to pick us up some grub and for whoever else has the munchies?"

"Damn, playboy," mentioned Mike, overhearing Nard. "Don't yo' man get some say-so in who should pick us up something to eat?"

"How? And in what? And plus, I kinda' figured it would be better if you and ol' girl spent a lil' private time together while me and Miss Felicia do the same. I mean, that is, if you don't mind, Carmen?"

"We sure don't, do we, Carmen?" intervened Felicia.

"Whatever you say, mentor."

"Felicia, you hungry?"

"YES! Thank you very much! A sista' do have an appetite," answered Carmen for her friend.

"You got that, shawty. Mr. Mike, be sure to handle that, aiight," replied Nard, while pointing at Carmen.

"No problem. Hold me down while I try to better know what I'm working with."

Carmen elbowed him in his side. Mike yanked the lower end of her shorts, lifting her foot off the ground. He held a small portion in his hand before she shook him loose.

"And Mike, be sure you don't bring me back no red meat or any pork."

"What are you, some type of vegetation or something?" questioned Carmen.

"The correct word is vegetarian, and no, I'm not."

"Know damn well that ass was raised up on poppin' grease and bacon strips."

"You're right. I can't lie. Me and bacon had numerous parties together when I was a youngsta'. That is, until I learned a lil' self-knowledge on how the bacteria in swine can destroy the body, along with the mind, and also how the process of digesting red meat is very complicated on the digestive system."

"Not only does this brother look good, but he's educated, too," stated Carmen.

The ladies exchanged high fives in approval of Nard's intelligence.

"You ain't know," informed Mike. "Me and my man both have diplomas and recently finished attending college in the past also."

"Thank you, Jesus," blurted Carmen.

"Thank you, Jesus! Oh, it's like that now? OK. Aiight, then. I tell you what…"

She detected his swift grasp at her arm and sprinted off. He gave chase around the parking lot until he caught ahold of her. Into the air, he lifted her, hearing loud screams and begs of him for her to be placed down.

"I guess it's just the two of us, Nard."

"I wouldn't want it any other way, you feel me."

"No," smiled Felicia.

"I'm sure you don't, being that a touch from my hands is just a short space away from your body."

"Are you flirting with me?"

"Who, ME? What makes you say that?"

"Just curious."

"Boys flirt." His quick instinct guided him around to the back part of her body. Studying her flawless figure, he whispered in her ear, "Men make moves." He placed a hand on her hip, allowing it to slide gently down her thigh. "Smooth ones at that."

"What are you…doing?"

Her voice had settled to a softer pitch. Eyelids in a sealant. She knew his behavior violated her space. Her body adored the way he manipulated her flesh. One of her key strengths was keeping a man at a distance without temptation overtaking her actions. Nard somehow managed to surpass those boundaries and she knew there was no turning back on his part.

"I'm helping you go with the flow."

"Is this," she said, her words paused by a brief sigh, "how you treat all your just-met female friends?"

"It's not me, cutie. It's the weed."

The punch he received to his stomach expressed her humor. He extended his face forward, inhaling the feminine fragrance that laced her neck. Her eyes widened as she felt his steaming heat flow from out of his nose onto her earlobe.

"I take it, the lovely smell that I'm smelling is a natural in-between-time and in-the-meantime odor for you?"

"Mmm hmmm."

His arms crossed behind his back, easing himself to a complete halt and rested up against the roundness of her derriere.

"Felicia, I got some bad news." Her ear slightly tilted closer to his mouth. "A brotha' has to use the restroom real quick right, but I hate to leave you out here like this all by yourself, feeling too relaxed."

Looking over her shoulder at him, she said, "And what are you suggesting?"

"That you quietly escort me in and out safely. You know, just in case the neighborhood robber man is out and about, lurking for his daily prey. I wouldn't be able to live with myself if something happened to your precious beauty while in the care of my responsibility."

"What if someone sees us go inside?"

"The bathroom is in the back."

"Meaning?"

"Meaning, the chances of us being spied on are slim to none."

"Has anybody ever told you you're too much?"

"Yeah. Just my mother, who's always telling me I'm too much of bullshit."

He went and locked the doors to his car. Something in her mind wanted to release his tight clasp as he led her in his direction. The more he escorted her, the less of a resistance her thoughts presented. It wasn't long before their appearance faded into the back of the carwash.

"I got a suggestion, Carmen. Rather a small one."

"What's on your mind, Mike?"

"How would you feel if you and your girls get with me and my man with a lil' mixture of parlaying at double D's tonight?"

"What's double D's?"

"One of the hottest spots on the outskirts of Columbus that never half steps. V.I.P. Live R&B/rap acts. You name it, they bring it."

"You mean Dime Dimensions."

"So you've been."

"Who hasn't?"

"Yeah, you might be right about that, but what I'm trying to do now is make sure between now and then that the two of us are well-acquainted and comfortable with our presence before any later events."

"Sure. As long as you don't leeeeean too hard to the right and get to know the streets better than you would like, everything else is everything."

She slanted her face at his, sharing a smile.

"I'm feeling that."

He checked himself over, locking the door.

"I'm sure you have some other females in your life."

"As well as you have other men, I suppose."

"Unfortunately, homeboy was very conceited, and arrogant as hell. The brotha' would stop by my place sometimes to pick me up and pranced in front of the bathroom mirror as if he was married to it or something for over an extended period of time, boasting about his looks. Anyway, that shit got real thin and eventually the midnight breeze came through and carried his ass away in the wind. Your turn."

"Well, I'll be lyin' if I said I was out here all alone, doing my own thang, but there's a twin I got who's my son and a baby mother who is about as crazy as that girl in the movie Fatal Attraction who couldn't take no for an answer when dude cut short the underground pipeline from her. What was shawty's name?"

"You mean Glenn Close."

"Yeah, yeah. That's the one."

"Have you ever thought that if you were at home being hubby that she might calm down some?"

She chose Captain D's as a reasonable choice of eatery. Mike had insisted on Red Lobster, but Carmen wanted to keep the spending range in its respectable area. She appreciated Nard's kindness, and to try to be greedy on someone else's generosity wasn't by far her character. A woman on the drive-thru intercom interrupted their dialogue. Her orders were brief, except for procrastination on the cheese stick she finally ordered for herself. "As I was sayin', you probably never even tried to, have you?"

"Before she got pregnant, shawty was cool as a fan. Matter fact, cooler than me! It's like, right after birth, all hell broke loose, wantin' nothin' but revenge on a brotha'. Beatin up on me. Burning my clothes. Food. The works. Other than that, we come and go as we please, but take extra good care of lil' man."

"What's his name?"

"Mike, Jr."

"Aaah, that's so cute."

"Not half as cute as you though."

He reached out, rubbing his hand over top hers that rested on the brake handle between the seats. A warm, comfort feeling flooded her heart. She placed her palm upwards and intertwined fingers with his.

"Oooooh…Nard…mmm…damn…baby…slow—"Felicia tried mentioning during their coitus, "—down…ssshit…"

"Since…I…eat…like…a…rabbit—"spoke Nard between his forceful strokes, "I…thought…I'd…sex…you…like…one…"

The latching sound to the bathroom door once it closed behind her meant she had actually gone too far. A one night stand in a bathroom stall where Nard patiently awaited her entrance seemed absurd. She did admire the cleanliness and how well-organized it was for public usage through all the turmoil. A swapping of kisses that ended faster than it started changed over into her leaning forward, feeling him unbutton her shorts from behind. Her mind completely shut down after feeling his first stroke slowly stretch her insides.

As the intercourse came to an end, her knees slightly buckled underneath her. She shoved him to the side, making a quick escape out of the stall. He watched her dress herself in front of the mirror.

"You know you are dead-ass wrong," she said, staring at him through the mirror.

"How you figga'?"

"Was it that good that it instantly put you into overdrive?"

"I'm sayin', it wasn't me, shawty. It was the—"

"I know, I know. It was the weed." He laughed at her reply. "That shit ain't funny, Nard. A sister can hardly even stand after being entered by Tarzan, the Ghetto Man."

He tried assisting her, but felt a resistance. She eventually gave in to his continuing tries. Their exit out of the bathroom together was noticed by Mike and Carmen in search of their presence. Felicia's feet came to an immediate stoppage. Carmen placed a hand over her mouth, startled by what revealeth in front of her eyes.

"Oooo-wee," mentioned Carmen. "Will somebody please pinch me and tell a sista' that I KNOW I didn't just see what I THOUGHT I just saw when I KNOW I got 20/20 vision and I AIN'T lyin'."

"NO, you didn't see, hear, nor are you going to speak anything to anyone."

She signaled to Felicia of her lips sealed in secrecy.

"Break it down who—" spoke Mike.

"The coolest cutta' at camp," finished Nard.

"Excuse me, Nard!"

"It's just my man actin' wild as usual, Felicia."

"Nard, can I talk to you? In private!"

"Excuse us, folks."

Felicia grabbed his shirt sleeve, forcing him to move in a hurry. Around the side of the building, they disappeared.

"Did you see anything, Mike?"

"Nah. Did you?"

"Just enough to make a sista' go—"

"And a brotha'," they harmonized together, "hmmmmmmmm."

Carmen guided herself into his arm, trying to quiet her laugh. Felicia stationed her hands at the base of Nard's shoulder, seeking his undivided attention.

"Now, where do we go from here, sir? Me, Felicia Jackson, somehow allowed you, a total stranger, to violate my space, which was a definite no. But, oh no, it doesn't stop there. I then allowed you to undress me shortly after we met, which was a bigger no-no. To make matters worse, we performed an act inside a public bathroom with a parking lot full of strangers, which REALLY was a no-no-no!" She dropped her hands to the side in disappointment at her carelessness. "Do I look vulnerable to you?" She awaited his answer. "HELL NO!"

"Are you surprised it happened?"

"AM I!"

"Maybe it happened because yo' body was tired of being deprived of what it's been missing from far too long. But if you want to, we can depart right now and act like this ordeal never took place."

"We both know that's impossible."

"Or, I can receive a piece of paper with yo' name and number on it and later on in the future I'll make a better attempt at smoothing out the rough edges."

"Promise me that you'll tell no one of what just happened between the two of us."

"A playa's promise."

"SAY WHAT, BOY!"

"I'm jokin', shawty."

"I'm serious, Nard."

"Aiight, aiight. I promise. Now, if you don't mind, can I get what I just asked for?"

"Be right back."

Her gait to the car displayed enjoyment more or less than disappointment. Nard slid back around to where they left Mike and Na-Na standing. Their entanglement exceeded beyond what they anticipated. Mike wasn't too fond of releasing her anytime soon unless she requested it. Na-Na felt the same. Her mind contemplated on their affair being one of different, more meaningful intentions and not just another guy wanting to jump in and out of her bed.

"Aiight, kids. Not in the public eyes," disrupted Nard.

"Not in the public bathroom either but it didn't stop the two of y'all."

"She might have a point there, Nard," agreed Mike.

Felicia soon returned, sliding a piece of paper in Nard's hand. She sprung upward on her tip-toes, planting a kiss on his lips.

"What was that about, shawty?"

"Nothin'. Just a see-you-later kiss. And make sure you use what's in your hand too. Come on, Carmen."

"Mike, walk me to the car so I can give you my info. Thank you for the food, Nard."

"Anytime, Carmen. And Felicia," gazing back at his lips, "nice meeting you."

She waved at him, increasing the pace of her walk. Mike made it back and posted up beside the passenger door.

"I don't even have to ask, do I, playboy?"

"Rule number one, definitely what you see with this cat is what you get," verified Nard.

They sat down in his car, digging off into the bag of food. A red light placed Carmen and Felicia's departure on hold in traffic. Carmen kept eyeing her friend, awaiting for a spillage on the incident that previously occurred. Felicia felt her staring, but refused to budge in Carmen's direction.

"Alright, girl! I can't take this silent treatment any longer! Come on with it! In full detail! Width? Length? Good? Bad? Best? Or worst?"

"The brother's utensil was rich, thick, and milk chocolatey."

"Melts in your hands."

"And mouth, if you want it to."

"Girl, you are as freaky as they come, Miss Undercover Lover." Carmen silenced her laugh, asking, "But there is one thing I gotta know."

"Which is?"

"Whatever happened to that remark you made earlier about keeping our coochies in the freezer before the heat melts them?"

"What can I say?" she said, turning to stare at Carmen. "Mr. Ice Cream Man saved the day."

CHAPTER: 6

Peaches recklessly raced past commuters, barely evading a bumper or side door. She knew her fast driving irritated D-Man and performed such careless act out of spite. He yelled at her numerous times over the past on respecting the speed limit, but the thrill of seeing her husband cringe gave her personal enjoyment. His request directed at her today carried no hostility in his voice, politely insisting of a reduction in their velocity. Startled by his unusual kindness, her foot eased up off the gas petal. She contemplated for a minute on the decision to continue driving normally when her foot instantaneously mashed down harder than before.

"I took care of that just like you said," confirmed D-Man while communicating on his Blackberry phone.

"All need to be sealed and safely out of harm's way ASAP," explained B.B. through the other end.

"Best believe it. 5.5 million stashed away out of this country, B.B." B.B., short for Big Boss, signified one of his top executives with the Columbian Cartel. The boss's whereabouts outside the country lingered between cocoa fields and guerilla warfare deals in the midst of Columbia's rain forest. "The rest shall be packed and delivered before the end of next week."

"Good. We don't need no forgetful American foolishness like the last puta' who thought he could hide along with my money without informing me."

She ran over a pothole. The phone slipped out his hand. He quickly retrieved it from his lap faster than it escaped him.

"B.B., hold on a second," he said, covering up the phone. "Woman, if you don't slow this bitch down, I'm gonna open your door and shove you out there into that traffic head first."

Screeching tires forced the car to a complete halt at a stop sign. The sudden force swung their heads forward just inches short of the windshield.

"Is that better?" she asked sarcastically.

He felt his anger surge and caught ahold of himself before he allowed his hands to damage her flawless skin.

"Remind me to hide you along with those damn keys when we get back home." His head jerked backward into his seat, feeling the strength of her Jaguar XF pull off. "As I was sayin', B.B., you know I can't speak for the next man's screw-ups but if you play to screw over someone, ten times out of ten a screwing is what you gon' get. In the asshole and on the lips."

"Hopefully he'll enjoy plucking daisies for the rest of his life."

"RIP, baby."

"And as for you, I'll tell you once. If you play the game with good intentions, you have my best wishes."

"Yes, sir."

"If not, grab ahold of your wife's ass and hold it tight cause that'll be the last woman on the face of this earth you'll ever touch again."

D-Man's heart slightly skipped a beat from the words his boss had spoken. He wasn't worried of mishandling his business but to hear such sincerity in B.B.'s voice told him just how deeply involved in the drug game has life had really become. The Cartel establishment towards any mistake made meant death to anyone responsible and possibly related to the victim. Children included. Peaches drove in silence, failing to get a glimpse of fear that laced his face temporarily.

"Until we talk again, B.B. Power is money."

The world through his eyes drifted back to years when he was younger. An adolescent whose craving for money inflamed his actions to partake in distributing small amounts of marijuana to local neighborhood customers. Uncle Charles had seen to Darryl learning the street trade with the possibility of one day running a family-oriented business. Darryl dared believed any harm could involve him relying on the reputation of his uncle once setting a man aflame over a one dollar bill or being acquitted on a murder charge for one of his former employees making a robbery attempt on him. Uncle Charles knew differently, supplying his nephew with protection, just in case. The two eventually agreed that the day would present itself where Darryl was actually living the truth or standing the chance of dying a lie.

"How come you always hangin' out with them guys older than you, Darryl?" Eddie demanded to know. "You know they ain't up to no earthly good."

"Tell 'em you hard-headed, Darryl. Go ahead, Jerome Darryl Jones! Tell 'em," repeated Shay-Shay.

"Cause they know how to shut up and keep they mouths closed, unlike you two."

"Look who's talkin'," spoke Shay-Shay. "If only you would've kept yo' mouth quiet about kissing my mouth, you probably could still be kissing it but NOOOOO, you had to tell this child with us who told Tony who told Stacy and lord knows how many million more kids know now after Stacy finished running her roadrunner."

"Hahahahahaha," laughed Eddie. "That was funny."

"I don't have to hang around you immature brats and listen to this mess."

"Boy, spell immature and I'm not talking about m, ma, and tour neither."

A long, gold 1976 Sedan Deville with tinted windows rolled up beside them. Thick clouds of smoke escaped the passenger window that slid down. Gray streaks of hair in Uncle Charles' beard stretched out the window. Darryl wasted no time approaching his relative. Shay-Shay and Eddie stood to the side, hoping he didn't jump in.

"Lil' cuzz, you still got that toy I gave you a few weeks ago, don't you?" Darryl patted the side of his shirt, where the butt of a Deringer 25 could barely be noticed. "Good. Cause the trap where we're about to ride to is like none other. These cats take pity on no one and I refuse to lose anyone, you feel me."

Darryl could only feel his heart pumping on the outside of his shirt. His past transactions were simple. But today, things had changed. The stakes were much higher. The money had increased. Along with problems.

"Come on. Hop in the backseat."

"DARRYL, DON'T BE STUPID ALL YOUR LIFE, BOY! YOU'RE ONLY THIRTEEN, NOT FORTY!" shouted Shay-Shay.

He paused a second before placing himself inside, acknowledging the truth in her words. The reflection in their eyes feared more than what he was experiencing. Through the windshield, he continued to watch his friends until they were only a speck. Seated alone on the huge backseat gave him a sense of loneliness. Similar to what his life had resembled for quite some time. His mother strung out on crack located across town. A father sentenced for life imprisonment with no chance of ever returning home. Not a trace of guardian supervision to watch out for him and instill any true values of life. Just his uncle sitting directly in front, who displayed some concern for him but mostly towards his money.

"You ready back there? Your toy loaded, ain't it?"

"Yep."

"Perfect. More than likely, you're probably going to need it. But our move will be the usual. You know, accept the cash first, make the pass, tilt the hat and then haul ass out of there. Try not to indulge in too many words. Be brief. Anything else is just trying to pick you apart. People are always searching for another weakness. Remember that. Aiight, we're here."

His sight revealed a yard full of spectators. Some in apparel worn over several weeks and in starvation. Empty bottles and cans were spread throughout the front lawn. Junk cars flooded the driveway.

A group of men laced in jewelry sat outside the entrance door, guzzling beers. Their commotion quickly grew silent, observing Darryl shut the door to the vehicle he exited. He double-checked his back pocket for the package, making his way to the house. One of the seated men tried addressing him, but kept silent until he made it in.

The inside appeared similar to the outside, if not worse. Roaches lay dead next to baseboards in corners of the living room, which spread an oily odor that plagued his nose. Areas of the house worsened the further he traveled on through. The sight of beauty in her face that flashed by him was only someone he could have only dreamt of. His senses got lost in thought as to what reason he had for being there in the first place. He only wanted to picture a part of his lonely life living in existence of her presence on a day-to-day basis.

"Who you here fo', boy? I SAID, who you here fo', boy!"

An elderly woman in a ragged nightgown stood in front of him. Her breath of a rank smell. He wiped his face of the lingering odor, hoping she hadn't put a permanent stain on him and stepped backward.

"To exchange out the one for the two, then three and four this thang out of here."

"That's what I'm talkin' 'bout. A kid I can dig."

Through her smile, she displayed discolored and decayed teeth. He felt relieved when she finally freed his sight and continued searching the house for the girl. The soft touches of someone's finger tapping him on the shoulder forced him to turn around swiftly.

"What's your name?"

Surprised at her sight, he responded, "Darryl. And yours?"

"They call me Star. Somehow, they say that I manage to shine through all this darkness."

"Why do you live here in such a hellhole?"

"I have nowhere else to go. And you?"

"I have somewhere, but it ain't much better than this."

"STAR! Get yo' ass in here! Right now!"

"My auntie called me. Sorry, but I gotta go. I hope to see you again someday."

"You will, Star. Real soon."

"OK, son. I got yours. Now let me get mines."

He slid the package out of his back pocket and into her hands. Before realizing his mistake, he opened the envelope and counted twenty-five one dollar bills instead of the twenty-five one hundred dollar bills that were supposed to have been inside. The envelope fell to the floor as he reached for his gun. He ran to the entrance door of a room where gambling was taking place, demanding the rest of the money she'd shorted him. They ignored his presence and continued rolling dices on top of a bed sheet.

"POP!"

A spectator at the foot of the bed fell a victim to the sound of his gun in the buttocks. Everyone stopped and gave him their undivided attention. "GOT-DAMMIT! I SAID I WANT MY MONEY OR THE NEXT ONE CATCHES IT IN THE HEAD!" A sealed envelope was thrown by the side of his shoe. He dared move first until he was certain everyone's eyes presented fear. Satisfied at the respect gained, he slowly bent down, ripping open the envelope, noticing a stack of twenty-five one hundred dollar bills.

"Everybody…have a nice day."

Darryl stepped away from the door and raced down the hallway. He barely caught a glimpse of Star inside another room. The gesture she made with her middle finger informed his mind of her part involved as a decoy, almost causing him to slip. His heart turned colder than he ever could imagine. Her actions proved him right: love and drugs resided in two different worlds, no matter the individual involved in them! Uncle Charles waited outside the car, gun in hand.

"What was that noise I heard, lil' cuzz?"

"Just some badass kids in there, playing with fireworks."

"And look who's talking. The baddest of the baddest. My lil' D-Man."

"D-Man…D-MAN!" Peaches interrupted his stare, which stayed focused through the passenger window for an extended period of time, awakening him to his aftermath. The blank look on his face shifted into a smile. "Are you ever planning on giving up the game?"

"Baby, must I show you this tattoo every time you ask me such a foolish question?" He shifted his body around, raising his shirt up. "CROSS MY HEART…NO TIME TO DIE…D-MAN'S GAME!" Greek letters engraved in and out of a huge cross on his back. She faced the road after watching her husband display his true existence. "You know I love you, right? All I ask is that you treat me the same way I continue to treat you."

She bit down on her tongue, trying to refrain from expressing her disgust involving his crime-infested life. Her recent pleas of him quitting his occupation went through one ear and out the other. The one to two week solo trips he began to take added further frustration as she worried herself senseless about his safety while halfway across the globe. He woke her this morning on his birthday, promising they would spend the day together, starting with his cookout she sped to at Lake Bottom Recreational Park.

Her exit out of the driver's side broadcasted impeccable beauty and vivacious curves placed in its uniqueness. The bell-bottom spandex she flaunted complemented her peachy skin tone. Upper attire exposed an excessive amount of cleavage. Fingers and toenails dazzled in pearly white polish matching her outfit. Gucci clogs with leather strings wrapped around her ankle helped soften her steps over a trail of gravel.

"Goooooood-damn!" 2-Piee shook his head in astonishment while she strolled past. "If that shawty was my shawty, I'd be one on-the-knees-begging-please type of brotha'."

"All day, every day," concurred J-Dub.

Their ogling lasted till her presence faded into a disappearance between the thickness of the crowd.

"Maaaaan," mentioned 2-Piece, playfully wiping his forehead. "I need a drink...AND a blunt. You wit' it?"

J-Dub's gullible expression clearly answered his friend's thoughtless question.

"I'll be a bigga' damn fool if I answered that, wouldn't I?"

The two knew of D-Man well before his status grew to an international drug smuggler. Around the time his hustling started migrating beyond Columbus, he recruited them as part of his founding clique, the "Entourage". His interest came soon after receiving word of a shoot-out involving 2-Piece saving J-Dub's life. They were outnumbered by a group of Jamaicans, three to one, demanding their territory. Both turned and walked away from the confrontation in laughs. Several shots had rung out. One hit J-Dub in the leg unable to make it to safety. 2-Piece knew that if his friend stood any chance of surviving, he had to be shielded in the middle of the street where he laid. He stationed himself atop of his friend and unloaded the twin nine millimeter Berettas he kept in his double shoulder holster. Their adversaries eventually fled in retreat. Such heroic events made major headlines throughout the entire city. D-Man made it his duty in taking a personal trip to consult about their needed assistance in his organization. The rules established were simple: BLOOD IN AND BLOOD OUT! 2-Piece couldn't contain his laughter once handed the Bylaws within the group. D-Man eyed him in anger, knowing 2-Piece would one day be a minor problem he would solve. He cleared the smirk off his face and regained his seriousness. A thorough handshake finalized the deal.

Peaches' arm rested around D-Man's waist, hearing him exert his male dominance to some friends. His thirty-five years of living lacked sign he was aging anytime soon. He avoided numerous invitations for parties throughout his adult life in hopes of suppressing the troubled childhood memories that often occurred. Lonely nights of tears streaming down his face in await to be greeted with cake and presents were unfulfilled. Her addiction before his birth continued up until his fifteenth birthday, having overdosed in a vacant house.

His celebration today felt less stressful. He forgave her, but his past would be a memory never forgotten, no matter how hard he tried. The chef catering the meal yelled, "SUPPER TIME!" interrupting his conversation. Lingering crowds dispersed and rushed to the grills. D-Man whispered in his wife's ear to prepare him a plate before he walked in the opposite direction.

"ENTOURAGE," shouted D-Man. "FRONT AND CENTER!" His employees followed him to a secluded area. "Listen up, due day for pay day is in two days."

The crew nodded in agreement.

"A D, I don't think I'll be able to have mines by then, man," spoke 2-Piece.

D-Man's heaving made his bulky chest raise dramatically.

"2-Piece," he responded in a huskier tone, "don't give me that same sob-ass story again, cause I done already let you slide one time too many, but not this time."

"Work with me, D! You know I can shake and bake but shit's been shady lately."

2-Piece stood and watched D-Man's larger frame approach closer.

"MOTHER—"he blurted before landing a solid blow to 2-Piece's nose.

CHAPTER: 7

Mike insisted on lounging at his place, which drew major doubts from his friend. Nard wanted first to finish off the blunt while cruising around before dealing with Shenequa's aggravation. The warning Mike shared was to be as cautious as possible once inside and remain on the living room couch only. He had hoped for Shenequa to have left, taking care of the errands she informed him of it this morning. Her car was still parked in the driveway, possibly having went with her friends. He opened the front door and couldn't move any further. Mike pleaded for an entrance, but was silenced at the gesture her hand made. She extended her arm outward, yanking him inside. Nard nose planted up against the slamming door on his way in. He listened in, hearing their footsteps trample down the hallway, and crept inside. His laughing accompanied him to a comfortable position on the couch.

"NEGRO," yelled Shenequa. She swung her hand at his shoulder, landing it on his neck.

"Damn, girl! Are you crazy!"

"You exactly right! Crazy for allowing yo' sorry ass to continue living in my got-damn house. Mike, you know damn well you was supposed to take lil' man to the park earlier today. Because of you, I didn't even get a chance to handle my business like I had planned to for today. What happened, sir?"

"Ah man, I honestly forgot, Shenequa. Is he mad at me?"

"What do you think?"

Lil' man crawled out of his bed, awakened by the disputing. He went into the living room and saw Nard seated on the couch, placing himself beside him.

"What's up with the sad look on y our face, lil' man?"

"My dad forgot to take me to the park to play with the swings."

"He did!"

"Yeah," he said, sounding somewhat saddened.

"Come closer and let me share a lil' somethin' with you," he said, placing an arm around his shoulder. "Do you actually think for one minute that your loving dad would mean to do such a horrible thing to a loving child such as yourself?"

"I don't think so."

"Listen to me and pay very close attention, okay. You see, sometimes, we adults forget to do important things for our friends and even family. I bet you forget to brush your teeth at times, don't you?" Lil' man nodded in agreement. "Do you mean to forget? No? Good. So what do we do to make sure we don't make the same mistake twice? We write it down or keep telling ourselves 'I won't forget, I won't forget'!" Nard tickled lil' man's side. He tried squirming himself free. "You do love your daddy, don't you?"

"Of course, Uncle."

The two stared down the hallway at Mike and Shenequa coming close to their proximity.

"Now go and show your daddy you're not mad at him and no matter that he forgot this one time, you still got plenty of love for him."

Lil' man sprung off the couch and into Mike's arms.

"I love you, daddy!"

"I love you too, son, and daddy will make it up to you as soon as possible. Okay?"

"Yes, sir."

"I don't know if you missed my greeting earlier, Shenequa, but I'll try it again. Hello, Miss Shenequa."

"Hello to you, too, Mr. Nard. Same ol' baby daddy drama on my end."

"Well, look here, momma, poppa, and junior bear, I gots to be sliding off to the crib to take care of some unfinished business. Poppa bear, do the right thang and I'll get back at 'cha in about several hours."

"Whatever is clever."

"Bye, Uncle Nard."

"Be good, lil' man. You too, Shenequa."

"Hurry up and get yo' butt out of here before I ban you from my house...FOR GOOD!"

She pointed at the door for him to make a quick exit.

CHAPTER: 8

Nard parked on the side of the curb, observing the continuation of his home in remodeling stages. A luxurious three-bedroom, double-car garage rested amongst wealthy suburbanites located in Quail Ridge Development of North Columbus. Painters were busy at work, painting the outer area a Carolina blue in white trimming, unaware of his presence. The dining and living room carpet was replaced several days ago with Italian rugs, covering a large portion of the wooden floor. At the last minute, he decided against installing a Jacuzzi and approved of a shower almost twice the size of the old one. A few other tasks in the kitchen and guestroom were to be completed before moving back in.

In the meantime, he'd regretted having asked his mother to be allowed back home temporarily until the minor scenario was resolved. Miss Hick found it somewhat amusing that her son would want to be under her roof, knowing how strict her house rules were. Day to day involvement of conflicts plagued his in and out departures, regardless of how well he behaved himself. She made it her duty in finding ways to challenge her son's patience in determining an improvement in their maturity or try detecting an internal growth of frustration which furthered her enquiry into the problem possibly arising. The games she played informed him of one thing: A mother's concern was always a mother's love. His entrance revealed a sight of her preoccupied with polishing her toenails. She spied his every movement inside the kitchen out her periphery.

"Wait a minute! Don't use that glass. Put it back. Special occasions only."

"Momma, you can't be serious."

"Drink out it and I'll show you just exactly what serious means." He hesitated a short moment in disapproval and placed it back on the top cabinet. "Grab one of them plastic cups at the bottom by your foot. And by the way, how much longer do I have of picking up this phone of mines that I paid for with my hard-earned money and telling those duck-duck-goose of yours who keep calling my house, 'no, he's not here and won't be back until Mork and Mindy return from Mars'?"

"The last time I consulted with them they said the house should be finished within possibly a week. I just stopped by, but only to check things out from a distance."

"Thank you, Jesus! Cause once it is finally completed, I'll let you have this wonderful home and phone of mines while I go and reside in your extravagant paradise."

"You wish."

"You damn right. Just like I had wish for you to have crawled back into my stomach as a baby but you didn't."

"By the way, has my boss left any messages? I haven't heard from him all day."

"Don't he got your cell number?"

"Yeah. But I still gave him yours just in case my telecommuni is somewhere thrown about of some shawty's place while daddy doing his thang."

He made a circular motion with his arms, pretending to be embracing the comfort of a woman.

"Like father, like son. But that's why his ass is single now. All because he didn't know when to say when." Her comment stung to his ear in serious concern of his father and the mistake possibly made. He slumped down in a seat, deciding to listen more to what she might have to say. "Son, listen. It'll hopefully come a time in your life when you'll realize that all you're doing is hurting the precious feelings of some young lady or wasting valuable time with your life when you could be trying to settle down, marry, and possibly raise a family. I know you might consider it as having fun or whatever you young leg-heads of today may call it but when the age starts creeping up on you like it does everyone else before they know it, who's gonna have your back?" She stared at him, answerless, responding, "Not me! Oh no! It's destined for your mother to be somewhere earth diggin' with the worms if you know what I mean."

"But I'm a man, momma," he expressed strongly. "I have a four-year college degree. Your son works as a car salesman for Mercedes that pays damn good AND to top it off, I have a house on the hill that's like that. Who could ask for anything more?"

"You still missing the point, aren't you? Why have all that material mess without being able to share it with someone you love? Like a wife. Or kids who can gloat over your achievements more than you do. That is, unless, you find Miss Palm Tree, your bride-to-be, irresistible."

She motioned her hand in a slow movement of ejaculation. His hard laughter caused him to gag.

"Never that," he responded.

"Well, I'd advise you to start thinking long term and do away with the foolishness. I don't mean to start right now, but to put it in that memory chip of yours because an overnight change would be even impossible for the Pope being caught in the bathroom sniffing coke." He sat in silence, pondering the truth in her words. At no point up to now had he given marriage or kids any serious thought. Living life, his life, to the fullest without the excess problems had been his only motive. Easily excluding himself from the "where you been" or "where you going" sort of harassments. Only doing as he pleases when he pleases. "And by the way, what's the purpose of having a cell phone if none of your women friends can get in touch with you?"

"Maybe because it's for more important business reasons with a small percentage of it for, as them street cats would say, 'Flossen'."

"Maybe that's why them street cats mainly eat off the streets and not at home too. Portraying to be something they ain't."

"It's possible."

"I know it is. And as far as these chicken heads constantly calling my house, you have twenty-four hours to caller ID and redial they butts cause come Monday morning, I'm changing my number. No ifs, ands or buts about it."

"Have I ever told you I love you, woman?"

"Yes, you have. Right before I would tear those lil' legs up of yours when you was a child." She continued applying polish to her toes. His bogus yarning distracted her none. "Move out the way, boy!" A startled look flooded her gleeful eyes, shoving him to the side after he snuck a kiss on her cheek. "I definitely didn't raise no tender-hearted son. At least I hope I didn't."

He walked out of the room way before he had a chance to hear her last comment made. His outfits were kept neatly pressed on hangers in the guest room closet browsing at a choice for tonight. One was tossed on the bed as he made his way to the phone. The dial tone echoed throughout the room from its speaker phone and punched in a few numbers. Mike's voice interrupted the first ringing sound.

"Yeah. What's up?"

"You! And the sun making its evening noon departure real soon. So gone and get yo' mind and time right cause it's about to go down."

"Everything is copacetic on my end. Shenequa and lil' man headed over to her mom's place in about an hour, leaving the rest to the left, you feel me."

"What's up with lil' man, anyway? You take care of that situation?"

"He cool."

"Good. Just make sure you get him to the park ASAP or it's you against my world."

"Whatever you say, big bra'."

"I'll be 'round soon. Peace out."

He made it back around to where the phone was quieting its dial tone.

CHAPTER: 9

Big Hick shook loose the hairs off his apron and viewed another customer take a seat in the master barber chair. Since opening hours of seven a.m., he'd been on his feet, refusing to break in hopes of clearing out the overcrowding inside. The clock on the wall read 3:49 p.m. and his ingrown toenail were wearing down terribly on him. T-Funk identified his brother's pain and continued cutting hair nonchalantly. The dream of one day owning their own barbershop presented itself at a bargain. Mr. Johnny Walker, who formerly owned the barbershop for the past thirty years, ended up falling in love with both heroin and a heroin addict. She somehow managed to convince Mr. Walker to sample the drug and from that point on, the sample became a habit and with the habit came a dwendling bank account of $100,000's to almost zero in an eighteen month period. Rent and other expenses had fallen behind. A letter labeled First National Bank delivered by USPS (United States Postal Service), stated to pay off the back taxes owed on the building within thirty days or face immediate foreclosure. Big Hick and T-Funk hadn't thought twice about taking over the operation. Together, they counted out two-thousand and five hundred dollars but were still five hundred dollars short. Slim insisted on pawning the title to his PT Cruiser to help come up with the remaining money. Their legal assistance finalized the deal for the three having complete ownership of the renamed business "Exquisite Cuts and Styles."

Additional usage of the place helped improve its clientele. The brothers offered the building when closed on Mondays for local businessmen to congregate towards betterment in the community. Bick Hick went to the weekly meetings in hopes of raising his two sons in a drug-free environment. T-Funk implemented free barbecue each spring on a once-a-month basis for the surrounding kids. The neighboring parents always supported his idea and contributed as much free time and effort as possible.

Nard requested a key of his own for late night rendezvouses. Big Hick granted his wish, stipulating an ultimatum of strict responsibility or be banned indefinitely. He seldom used the place except for a last minute resort. A blanket spread out on the floor and her body lowered softly down atop of it helped ease some of her doubts.

"What do you think we're about to do on that Nard?"

"Oh, this shawty? Trust me, Motel 6 ain't got nuthin' on A'la Quilt, the comfy."

In the end, soft music with mellow drinks had her wanting again to reconvene their togetherness at the same location.

The commotion carrying on in the shop was hard for Big Hick to ignore from being nosy as usual. He made sure the customers kept him informed on the good, bad and ugly daily. On and off sounds of clippers echoing in the background continued to justify the reason tips were plentiful and "thank you"'s were a normal ritual.

"Mr. Funk, I forgot to tell you earlier that I bumped into Nard out on the eastside of C-town this morning," informed Slim.

"Maaan, that lame be fakin' hard."

"Who that, Funk?" questioned Big Hick, overhearing their dialogue.

"Yo' brotha'…Nard."

Big Hick inquired, "On what grounds?"

"Fo' impersonating his lil' bra' on that real playa' flave."

"I don't know Funk," spoke Slim. "The word on the streets out these shawtys' mouth is that you could easily win the poo-nanny pie eating contenst."

"Damn you," replied Funk.

"Coochie eating! Playa' shit! Pardon my French, gentlemen."

"No," stated Big Hick. "Pardon everyone from saying, on three fellas…one…two…three…OOOOOH SHIT!"

"What y'all mean 'ooooh shit'," protested 7-0. "Boy, I tell you what, go and ask yo' mothers who granted them permission to go out and play in the park after it got dark."

"What you should be asking yo'self is who allowed you to step outside in that early 1800's outfit you wearing over there," responded Big Hick.

The topics discussed lately forced 7-0 to express his own experience. To sit and be unheard possibly meant catastrophic results by the youth if not properly informed; in his reserved seating off to the back he read the USA Today in silence on noon Saturdays. His frail limbs and short height didn't take much to be hidden behind the extended paper he held on to. A heavy pitch in his scratchy voice were clear signs of struggles he had endured for sixty odd years. Big Hick continued welcoming his presence long after his best friend no longer owned the place of business. He stood up and tucked the folded paper underneath his armpit. His shirt wiped free of any crinkles. Most of the customers laughed at the seventy-style suits he wore, having been branded the name seven pronounced with the letter 0, which bothered him none.

"Son," he said, brushing the lint off his pants, "this style is what made y'all young whippa' snappa's think y'all smoother than me today. The real O.G. of the game."

"More like original garbage," teased Slim.

"Gone head. Get yo' jokes off but I'll tell you this. I could let all of y'all and some, go and indulge in sex with any female of your choice and I bet you I can come right behind you and touch one spot on her body that'll instantly drive her up the wall and I promise you, she'll act like you never existed."

"Be serious, pops. Who do you think you are? The wizard of thongs?" questioned T-Funk.

"Not at all. More like the man of understanding."

"What is it to understand? You take her clothes off, stick it in, and after a few minutes…it's over."

"Young man, a woman is waaay much more than sex but I wouldn't expect you to know that being you're so young, dumb, and with a mouthful of cum."

"We also understand," informed Big Hick, "that 280-Bypass has a gang of clothing stores that can easily bring yo' dress code back to the future 7-0."

"I tell you what, **BIG SHITTY**, you just continue to freak them chocolate cakes of yours that keep telling you lies about being the sexiest cake lover they ever met."

The laughter in the shop exploded into an uproar. Big Hick reared back on his stand and smiled.

D-Man stormed up a flight of stairs inside his two-story home in rage. Peaches kept silent the entire drive back from the cookout. She wanted to confront him about the violent act but decided to wait until he settled down. He paced back and forth in his spacious bathroom in deep contemplation. His tempered demeanor regained its composure in front of an eight-by-eight foot mirror beside the shower. No trace of scars were detectable on his face or bare chest. He strolled out in his boxers and house shoes, positioning himself on the bed, where she laid. She sat up on her knees, massaging his shoulders.

"Why did you have to make such a drastic scene today at your own cookout, baby? You know he wasn't no match for you."

"The youngsta', for some odd god-damn reason, keeps tryin' to play me, D-Man, as if I'm soft or getting' too old to whoop some ass."

"You did look kind of cute out there, slapping that boy around."

"Please, no autographs."

"Don't go getting the big head on me."

"Two big heads are better than one."

"Which reminds me, it's been a while since I felt the swelling of big head number two pushing inside of me."

Her hand crept its way down his hard abs to a resting place inside his boxers.

"Well, maybe it's time Tina Twat got beat down by Dick Turner, then."

She removed her hand out between his legs and lowered him down on the sheets. Her salacious gaze pierced through his eyes, a sight of anticipation beyond control. Without warning, her lips pressed gently to his. Their tongues entwined for a brief moment before she pulled herself back to an upright position. In a swift movement, her breasts were freed out of their temporary imprisonment. D-Man's pupils became enlarged at the first sight of their roundness dangling in the air above his head.

His entire frame slid onto the bed. Her face snaked its way past his forehead down to a spot on his chest. His tongue whirled around her nipple that lingered above his mouth. Her lips slid lower down his torso. She stopped at his boxers in search of his phallus through the slit with her hands. He slid her thong aside that rested against the base of his chin, extending his tongue outward over her clitoris. The warmth of her mouth smothered his limpness in starvation.

"How does it taste?" asked D-Man.

"Mmmmm-hmmm," moaned Peaches.

The lowering and raising of her head continued for several minutes.

"Hold on. Something ain't right," mentioned D-Man. "It hasn't ever taken this long for me to get an erection."

Her head lifted, and she stated, "The damn thing won't even get hard! WHY?"

"Shiiit, I don't know."

"The hell if you don't! If you'd keep it in my mouth and mine alone, we wouldn't be having this problem."

She jumped off the bed and stormed inside the bathroom, slamming the door. D-Man sat up at the end of the bed, somewhat perplexed at her unnecessary behavior.

"Bitches," he stated to himself.

CHAPTER: 10

Nard went by his home in exchange of the convertible for his four-door Mercedes Benz SCL 600, which displayed "D-P-WAY" on its license plate. His reconvening in traffic placed him and Mike back on schedule, having witnessed the daylight shift into the evening skies. Mike's head nodded in rhythm to the great lyrics of Michael Jackson's "Billy Jean" while eyeing spectators they passed in the downtime district. A flashing thought of the mistake he made earlier reminded him of just how careless he was at times. He wasn't convinced lil' man fully accepted his apology and it bothered him deeply. It dawned on him how marijuana might've been the blame for his forgetful action after thirteen years of its usage. The smoking habit he had would one day have to be put to an end, but he also knew that day was still far off.

"You know what, Mike, I was just wondering, right, and forgive me if I sound out of place for asking you this, but how the HELL do you and Shenequa manage to continue living together with all the turmoil y'all take each other through? And try to be as frank as you possibly can about answering that, too."

He gawked over at Nard, stating, "Elementary, my dear."

"You right. Elementary and some junior high school shit, too."

"But seriously, though. The real key ingredient of it all is to let her do her."

"As in let her sex whoever, whenever?"

"Hell nah, man. You see, a woman lives off of emotions as we playa's live off the notions."

"Meaning?"

"Meaning that, when it comes time for the real feelings to intertwine with hers, I never half-step. Rather, she's in the mood for a serious conversation about something or her body is calling for big daddy at three in the morning, I'm there. And as far as the pushing and shoving goes, majority of that is caused by my stupidity most of the time for being inconsiderate or just plain ol' doing dumb shit. I don't know."

"In other words, you jive know what to expect as well as she does."

"Somewhat."

"Sort of like a brotha' and sista' growing up together always picking at each other but at the end of the day, it's all love."

"Now you're thinking." Their dialogue discontinued momentarily. "And what's with all the questions anyway? The game startin' to weigh down on you or something? Yo' palms startin' to hurt? I mean, what's up?"

"Ain't nuthin'. I was just wondering why you be takin' all those ass whoopings so much. That's all. On the serious tip though, just some bs I was hearing on TV while tryin' to get dressed 'bout relationships and how to maintain one."

"Anyway," he said, brushing off the topic, "are you slippin' or is we trippin'?"

"What's up?"

Mike searched the pockets of his jeans for the blunt he rolled up at home.

"We been doing all this riding without any mind enhancer that we gots to be trippin' off of something."

"I was just waitin' for you to bring in the intro of some of that funky stuff."

"Say no more. I got the lighter, but," he fumbled around in his pockets, "what I…do with the——" He remembered placing it in his sock. "Here she is, homeboy. But like I was sayin', whatever it is that got that mind of yours all out of focus, one thang's fo' certain, the doc does have a cure for that ass." Undecided on whether or not to light it himself, he followed his second thought and passed it over, granting Nard the pleasure. "By all means, partna'. Smoke til' you choke."

He used his knees to steer the car and took hold of the items with both hands. An extended pull off the blunt reddened his eyes fast. The thick cloud of smoke exhaled out of his mouth barely permitted a view of Mike's smile on his face. Mike reached over, securing the steering wheel Nard's knees left unattended. He struggled, trying to clear his vision and regained control of the car.

"OK...OK! You wanna play rough," he mimicked Al Pacino's voice in Scarface. "Say hello to my lil' friend for me!" He held the blunt up, enjoying the effects of its stimulation.

They arrived at Exquisite Cuts a little after closing hour. The darkened parking lot was empty, which allowed them continuation of smoking. Big Hick was finishing off the last customer inside. Slim's hands were preoccupied with sweeping the remaining hairs off of the floor. He exchanged the broom for a Corona beer out of the small refrigerator located in the lounge room and positioned himself in his barber chair.

"A lil' nip here. A nip there," observed T-Funk in the mirror. "Oh yeah, can't forget to knock a lil' off the beard." He rotated his head from side to side, agreeing with his work. "Now this, my friend, is why we're known for our exquisite taste."

"Get it right, cat-daddy," informed Slim, "cause the moves to be made ain't that far away."

"It's only right that I get thangs tight. Who knows, I might run across some famous chic while parlaying at double D's tonight and the first thang she gon' check fo' and that's to see if the hairline is proper. After that, everything else is easy takin' for the makin'."

"Well, don't you think it's 'bout time you tightened up that tab of yours you been owing to that cash register for quite some time now," mentioned Big Hick. "So make sure you don't forget it cause me knowing you, you'll be sharin' all with them broads of what's left of yo' finance without romance, which is a dam shizzame'."

"Damn Funk! Is it any part of the game you do official without breaking any playa' rules?" enquired Slim.

"Most definitely. I'm always leavin' them freaks on they knees, feelin' weak, screamin' 'please, please papi, no mas, no mas'," expressed Funk.

"I might can give you a cool point fo' that one," sided Slim, "but only because you're kenfolks."

The chiming sound of bells overhanging the entrance door altered their attention.

"We're closed," yelled Big Hick.

"Hold on, Big Hick. It's yo' boy, Mike. What's up, baby?"

"Ah, shit, Mike. What's happenin', cuz?"

"Ain't nothin'," he said, exchanging hand greetings with Big Hick. "Funk, Slim, what it do fellas?"

"What up, shawt dawg," replied Slim.

"And look who's behind him, the pimp with much simp," teased Funk.

Nard strolled right up to his face.

"Watch yo' tongue, son, or daddy won't be schoolin' you no mo' on how not to be a Captain Sava', Mr. Sava'." The two's embrace was short. "Fat boy! I see that ham sammich hangin' out yo' back pocket is still in place."

"Yep. Just like those garlic ass gums of yours still killing off vampires too."

Slim stated, "So you made it through, Nard."

"It was only right I swang this way before headin' off into the night. Give us gents some time to step our game up before we hit the spot tonight. Believe me, if that mouthpiece ain't sweet, play it Funk way and drop bills at them hoe's feet."

"That's how do you it, bra'? Sprinkle salt all around a real playa' like me? I can't help it, my game is gold and yours been sold...out, that is."

"It's yo' world, pretty boy. I just live in it," spoke Nard.

"Well," said Slim, raising up to his feet, "I gots to go S-3 me."

"S-3? Could you please be more specific, sir," questioned Mike.

"You know, shit, shave, and shower. I'mma catch y'all at double D's later on."

"Hold up a minute, Slim. I need to holla' at you about somethin'."

Mike trailed him out of the door. Big Hick stretched in his chair as far back as it would recline. He hurriedly slid off both his shoes relieved the work day had finally come to an end.

"Check this out, Nard. If a snake was to bite me on my leg, what would you do?" asked Big Hick.

"I couldn't even tell you,, big bra'. I'd probably try to suck the venom out, added with a lil' hot sauce, mistaking it for a piece of chicken or somethin'."

"How about you, Funk? What if a snake was to bite me on the ass, what would you do?"

"One thang's fo' certain and two thang's fo damn sure, you'd definitely be one dead individual without no money in yo' pockets cause me and my ladies gotta eat to live. Now, if you gents don't mind, I gots to be headin' out that door myself to finish freshening up at the crib. Get at y'all later."

"Will I see you waddling across the dance floor tonight like some escaped walrus?" joked Nard.

"Nah. I doubt it. Big bra' is tired. Plus, I got to watch the kids tonight while they mother at church. So she tells me."

"Just keep an eye on the prize. I'mma bout to slide like grease and make sure you tell the family I said what's up."

"You got that. Hold it down."

A thin trail of smoke drifted past his nose just outside the door. He searched around, trying to detect the direction the burning aroma came from. It thickened in the silhouette on the side of the building. He crept in its direction, noticing everyone who left out huddled up close.

"Can I hit," asked Nard, snatching the blunt out of T-Funk's hand, "that blunt?"

"Watch out, boy! All you had to do was ask. I ain't got no problem with seeing you smoke your brain cells away."

Slim said, "Can't we all just get along?"

Nard inhaled several times and passed it back to T-Funk.

"You 'bout ready to do this, homeboy?"

"I'm waitin' on you, Mike."

"Slim, T-Funk, holla' at y'all two tonight."

"True that, Mike," responded Slim.

T-Funk stated, "Catch me with the big boy cigar, actin' like big boy stars, being sweated from afar by them all."

Nard mentioned, "Just as long as Big John ain't the one sweatin' that backside from the back side of the club." T-Funk rushed his brother and grabbed ahold of him. "Cut with the jokes, son!" Nard struggled to free himself loose out of his brother's clasp. "Chill out before I get dirty, boy."

Their horseplaying came to a cease. They made an exit out of the parking lot.

"Girl, I sure as hell hope you ain't pick me up just to be ridin' around with yo' ass all night long all because Mike done left you stranded, as usual, again and again and again. If so, you could've left me at home, picking loose the dead hairs between my ass, which would probably be more fun than what we're doing right now. Ridin' around, lookin' fooler than foolish," informed Tosha.

"One thang about it, miss broke and lonely. All you have to do is wait til' we turn off on this highway up the road, open your door in mid-traffic, and politely step out. It's just that simple. If not, sit yo' fast tail down and enjoy parts of the city you only get to view once or maybe twice a year," reproached Shenequa.

"Well, I guess she told you, Tosha," enlightened Meka.

Uncertainty of a location started the usual strife amongst Shenequa and Tosha. Meka enjoyed her friends' constant dispute, having no merits whenever they gathered together. Tosha pushed her weight around occasionally, but kept it in perspective the majority of the time. She reached between the front seats, snatching a bottle of Hypnotiq and vodka out between Meka's legs. Meka slung several plastic cups back at her, demanding full service in having them filled. Tosha broke the seal off the bottle of vodka and took a gulp.

"Goooooood gracious! This stuff is dangerous! Where the water at?" She fanned her scorching mouth.

"You see, that's what yo' greedy ass gets," said Shenequa.

"Woman, what you about to get is some wet seats if you don't stop somewhere real soon so I can use the bathroom cause my bladder is tickling the shit out Miss. Cliti," said Tosha.

"Damn, girl," stated Meka shockingly. "You that bagged up from gettin' you some that yo' piss is giving you the itch?"

Shenequa eyed her from out of the mirror overhanging the dashboard, shaking her head in disbelief.

"Just don't start pissing and cumming on my seats cause I just cleaned this used-to-be-dirty thang up."

"Whateveeeeeeer," responded Tosha.

"By the way, girls," she said, positioning her body around at Shenequa and Tosha, "I heard it through the grapevine while hanging out at the mall earlier today that Dime Dimensions is supposed to be packed beyond capacity tonight. Some famous artists supposed to be performing."

Shenequa warned, "We can't go there."

"Why?" fretted Meka.

"Cause, the rules are, if that ass ain't fine, no inside, and we just can't leave Tosha out in the car all night by herself."

"Bitch," pointed Tosha at Shenequa's head, "don't make me slap yo' ass."

Her backhand placed to the side of Shenequa's face, laughing. Their gibberish faded off into traffic, rocking the small car from left to right.

CHAPTER: 11

An overview of Dime Dimensions displayed an extended line of vehicles swarming the lot. Neon lights glared brightly above the entrance doors, signifying its dominant status amongst competition. Nard's speedometer bounced in the range of five and ten miles, traveling alongside of stagnant traffic down the wrong lane. A motorist up ahead permitted him enough room to station his ride in a parking space that became available. Mike raced to the trunk and prepared another dosage of blended cognac. They sat, spying women dressed in skimpy outfits, waiting in line to enter. A scenery of pushing and shoving off to Nard's left quickly preoccupied his sight.

He took several swallows out of his cup, stating, "You see this dude here? That dude right there. You see him?"

Mike's eyelids were rested shut, unaware of anything. The top part of his head was barely visible to passersby while reclining in the seat. Nard eyed over his shoulder, awaiting a response.

"Damn negro," he said, rubbing his nose Nard had squeezed. "Chill with that dumb shit you on."

"Look, fool!" He pointed at the woman in denial of having some young man preoccupying her space. "Now you see, this dude here, has what you might call the 'oh no' syndrome."

"Cut with the jokes, man."

"Seriously! I bet you a hundred dollars right now that she's tellin' him, 'oh HELL no you ain't with me tonight'."

"Well, me personally, I think it's 'bout time these shawties recognize a real one." Mike jumped out of the car with his hands to the sky, shouting aloud to no one in particular. "HAAAAAAY-HOOOOOS!"

"Close my door, fool," he said, extending an arm over, placing his passenger door shut. "You lettin' all the fresh leather scent out. I'm sorry 'bout that, baby," he said, massaging his passenger seat. "The boy wasn't raised too bright."

Mike placed himself alongside of a young lady on her way inside. His hand grabbed hold of hers, acknowledging the confused look she displayed.

"Excuse me, miss, but is a brotha' being a tad bit rude by trying to get to know you on such an unexpected approach?"

"Say what?" she expressed irritably.

"Mike. And you are?" He released her hand.

"Tonya."

"Well, Miss Tonya, is it possible that I've made my presence known a lil' too early, seeing that the night is young with you probably wanting to have much fun. But if my timing is right and your mood is nice, I take it we'll be bumping and grinding into each other all through the night."

"Maybe."

"Sooo does that weigh more in favor of a yes?" He leaned his body in plea.

"I guess so. But only if you allow me to escort you in."

"By all means," he said, pulling her body close to his.

Nard caught a glimpse of Mike before he disappeared inside the building. His fast maneuvering through the crowd, trying to catch up, came to a sudden halt, caused by two huge women in his path, refusing to budge out of the way.

"I see you, homeboy," he mentioned under his breath, still in blockage.

A trio of heads hung outside of car windows circling the parking lot. Honking the horn foolishly and loud shouting at no one in particular drew their biggest scenery thus far. The large throng somewhat lowered their commotion, watching the women continue to be of a disturbance as they drove past. Tosha yelled for Shenequa to hit the brakes. Her words intervene a couple's dialogue on the side she hung her head out of.

"That's right! You see me! The baddest thang yet! So how 'bout get in where you fit in with me, homeboy, somewhere on this backseat, instead of being turned into stone by Medusa's auntie you hangin' out with." His pants slid down and he spread his butt cheeks apart directly at her face. "What the! Nigga! You ain't all that Slim Grady! Shady! Or whatever it is you portrayin' to be with yo' ashy ass. Did y'all see that?"

"Not only did we see it but did you believe it?" laughed Shenequa.

"Hell nah! He really must have me mistaken for some ghetto trash."

"You are from the projects, right Tosha?"

"Yeah."

"With a raggedy screen door, right?"

"Yeah. And?"

"And, if I'm not mistaken, roaches do come out at night where you cook your food to. I mean, are you with me yet or do I need to go a lil' further? Let me know cause if not, there must be a newer description to your lifestyle of the poor and hazardous."

"Come on, you two goonettes," interrupted Meka. "All these fine-ass brothas out here and y'all wanna bicker and beef with each other like two old hags."

"You could be right," agreed Shenequa, placing her attention back to the scenery. "There is a lot of good lookin' brothas out here."

"Have you not forgotten MISS THANG?" informed Tosha. "Not only are you not free to be but you AND your man has a child. AND living together."

"And what exactly ARE you insinuating?"

"That, that ass of yours is definitely ain't fo' the takin'."

"You right. This body ain't for the takin' but it's damn sho' fo' the shakin' which is exactly what I plan on doing."

She twirled her arms around in unison of her hips, anxiously awaiting the dance floor.

"By the way, Tosha," enlightened Meka, "don't be up in here tryin' to cut in on those couples already preoccupied on the dance floor. Find you somebody that's just lingering around playin' the wino man or something."

"Forget them hoochie mommas! Can I help it if I get jealous too easy when I see some sexy male figure dancing with some 'thang' that thinks she's all that?"

"Don't start none and it won't be none, Tosha," informed Shenequa.

"All I want to know is, if one of them broads gets out of line am I covered from front to back?"

To her surprise, they acted out the answer Tosha awaited to hear.

"FRONT! BACK!" They finished their chant with a dance swing. "AND SIDE TO SIDE!"

"Thaaaaaank youuuuuu," expressed Tosha with gloat.

CHAPTER: 12

The club capacity neared its peak of almost one thousand inside. Security guards double-checked partygoers at random after clearing metal detectors. Dim blue ceiling lights beamed through the thickness of cloudy smoke and darkness. A rectangular-shaped dance floor made of thick fiberglass exceeded two to three feet above ground level in the center. Wooden rails circled its borders, keeping dancers in safety. Several dance groups partook in a contest at a chance of signing on as an opening act for a major artist or group while on tour. Their performance captivated the majority of the spectators, receiving numerous amounts of "ooooh"s and "aaaaah"s. DJ 1NE requested through the music for serious crowd participation in favor of a possible winner.

Further activities carrying on at the bar presented an act of three-bottle juggling, performed by a bartender. He drank out of each one when their opening faced downward in the air. A round of applause was shared as the trick came to an end. He stumbled backwards in his steps, displaying a sign of drunkenness. Drinks were ordered through another bartender, who continued finding humor in his friend's circus behavior for as long as the two had worked together.

An area off to the far corner guarded by two huge men monitored the in and out entrance to the VIP room. Tonight's special guest prepaid in advance, but was refunded his money. Instead, homage went in favor of the one man responsible for establishing Dime Dimensions and its success. D-Man's past investment in the club helped launch a variety of opportunities for up-and-coming talent surrounding Columbus and Phenix City. Nard eyed inside at the gorgeous women dancing around. His solid stare was broken up by one of the huge men posted outside signaling for him to look in a different direction.

Nard moved onward through the fog of smoke he tried fanning from in his face. He shortened his walk besides the wooden rails and felt a soft touch of taps on his arm. "Hey, good-lookin'." Her spoken identity pressed against his earlobe informed him who she was without having to look.

"Do I know you?" he jokingly teased.

"Do you know me?" She moved from beside him to in front of him.

"Ooooh, Samone! It's just that, your hair, it looks so…different. But in a tempting way. Somewhat makin' it almost impossible for me to identify with the beauty that stands in front of me."

"Thank you but no thank you for that lame-ass compliment of yours."

"So what's been up with you? The last time we spoke you and your soon-to-be future husband was off and running to Viva Las Vegas."

"Times change. As well as people. Instead of growing closer, we grew further apart. But that's not important. You are."

"Which exactly was the next question I was just about to ask you. Are you enjoying yo'self or have I just brightened up the party for you?"

"How'd you guess?"

"Cause by the looks of thangs, it's written all over your face."

"Could you read what else it's saying?" she asked in a flirty manner.

"Let me guess." He placed a finger just below his temple, pretending to be dumbfounded at her question. "That, before the end of the night, you hope to see the two of our bodies somewhere tangled up doing what we used to do best."

"Bingo!"

She moved in closer, filling the space that once separated their bodies and rested against his.

"I tell you what, right, give me some time to think on it and I'll definitely let you know something."

"Don't take too long, big boy, cause you're not the only one in the club, shedding light on this subject."

Her delicate grip over his entire crotch area made him weaken at the knees, watching her smile and walk off. He soon regained his composure, shaking loose the freaky thoughts. Mike crossed his path long enough for them to salute each other and continue their separate ways. Nard noticed an available stool at the bar, speeding for its emptiness. The leather soft cushion gave in perfectly to his weight. Its fluffiness reminded him of the seats he not too long ago preoccupied. His hand went aloft, signaling for a drink.

"What's poppin', playa'?"

Mike bumped up against him, sliding onto an empty seat.

"I see yo' work, Casanova."

They spun around, facing the crowd.

"So far, so good for the home team, you know."

"Yeah, I'm sure it is with you showin' them shawties out there no slack at all."

"I mean, can you blame me? Not only is it open game and not for the lames, but shawty want a change and who's better equipped than us certified playa's?"

"Slay on, then playa'." He scanned the entire room. The angered commotion outside of VIP lasted briefly. "Why would anyone in their right minds want to scold that dime piece he's standing with? It just doesn't make any sense."

Mike caught a glimpse, responding, "Look here, playboy. Before you go getting' any crazy ideas, don't even think about it. That brotha' she's with is her hubby, D-Man, who is of no joke. And on top of that, you're steppin' out yo' league. Waaaay out yo' league."

"Way out my leage, you say? I'm sayin', how you know so much about the man they call D-Man?"

"Have not you forgotten? I live with a walking encyclopedia that's always keeping her big ears glued to the streets."

"That's very good to know, then, Mr. Mike, cause I ain't in the mood for joking nor playin' with Mr. D-Man."

Nard brushed a hand over his beard, watching D-Man zoom past his wife in the direction of the front entrance. A strong tug at his wrist withheld the glass he raised towards his lips.

"Hello, Tarzan," greeted Felicia.

"Hello to you too, Miss Beauty."

She leaned forward and embraced him in her arms.

"What's up, Mike?" spoke Carmen.

"I see you and Felicia made it."

"Do you actually think I would miss Libra featuring C-Beazy perform 'The Playa's Way' live and in plain view?" asked Carmen.

"All you have to do now is let me know when you're ready to see me get it crunk."

"Oh really?"

"You ain't know," intervened Nard. "My man was once the dance hall king on the floor."

"And no, I didn't. But there's only one way to find out."

DJ-1NE silenced the music mid-song. The room darkened to a pitch black. Frantic screams erupted for a short span. Several stage lights lit up a small portion of the club. Libra's heads hung low in stillness. An uproar of cheers exploded to the high-pitched sound coming from the lead singer's voice.

Carmen excitedly mentioned, "Ooooh shit, girl! That's that jam! Come on, Mike!"

She pulled at his shirt to accompany her.

"A brotha' must mention Carman that a playa' don't dance. He grooves."

"A playa' ain't a playa' without his females to pay with, either," rectified Carmen.

Mike stared over at Nard, saying, "She's got a point there."

"What you waitin' on, then? Handle yo' business," informed Nard.

He hesitantly stood to his feet. Carmen met his stance and entangled her arms around his.

"Look at them two fools, Nard. Crazy as they wanna be. And how about you, sir? What are you planning on doing? Staying glued to your seat all night?"

"Not really. But I figured it would be best if I stayed back, holdin' down my drink."

"So that means you don't want to feel my body up against yours, I suppose." She slithered in between his legs and removed the glass out of his hand, taking a sip. "SHIT! What is that?" she demanded in disgust.

"That, my dear, is what you call a straight-to-the-heart without any part of a chaser...Dr. Bom Bay."

"Drinking that stuff, you definitely gonna need some type of medical assistance once you finish."

"But if you wanna go out and shake that beautiful body of yours, enjoy yo'self. I'll be aiight."

"You sure?"

She felt his hand rest itself at the lower crease of her left buttock. "I'm positive."

Whispering in his ear, "Our party has just begun," she slid herself away.

Her departure was met by some guy not far from where she left Nard. She looked back at him, noticing the smile on his face, and the raised glass he held onto. He nodded his approval of the gentleman she was with who was requesting a dance. She thought it was awkward that he had okayed a complete stranger in her arms, and not him. She preferred Nard. Her signs were clear, but she went along with the program anyway.

"COMING THROUGH! COMING THROUGH! LADIES FIRST, YOU WITCHES! LADIES FIRST!"

Tosha bogarted her way through a small crowd conversing a couple yards past the metal detectors. Her friends trailed, sharing pushes and shoves of their own. In a similar stance, the three ladies observed the party mongers enjoying themselves.

"Look at those nasty lil' whores out on the floor. Their mothers would be ashamed of themselves if they knew their daughters were in here, performing such lewd acts on these men," said Tosha.

"Did you say nude or lewd, because one act seems to be leading into the other," responded Shenequa.

"When both halves of your ass are in the lap of four men at one time, well then...club dancing, I do not want to be a part of," explained Meka.

"Tss, tss, tss, my children," said Tosha, hugging her friends. "Now let's quit with the bs and shake all of what we got faster than a salt shaker."

She stepped off, vanishing into a crowd of waving hands.

Nard spied her loneliness off in the distance. Various men approached with small talk, but were baffled by her harsh rejections. Even a simple greeting of "hello" aroused her displeasure. That neither frightened nor discouraged the agenda he'd established for her early on. He tipped the bartender before departing. In a snail's pace, he moved in closer. Closer. He cleared his throat. Words escaped afterwards, and her eyes widened with rage.

"Forgive me if I'm wrong, but from the looks of things, either you're dissatisfied with the choice of men or somewhere not too far off is a man who is happily blessed to have entered the club with you, and hopefully leave with you as well." She fixed her mouth to respond, but was denied the chance. "But before you tell this fly to shoot, it's only right that you hear this for the one-thousand, one-hundred and one time...you are very beautiful."

A hastened response exited out of her mouth.

"Thank you for the compliment, but I don't think my husband would appreciate it."

She dared wait for his response before turning to face the crowd.

"A brotha' can detect a lil' hostility in your voice. Are you okay?"

Her grimace met his face.

"Sir, do you really want to know, or are you steady trying to get some type of conversation out of me before I tell you to get the hell out of my face?"

"Yes and no to your two-part question," he said, contemplating his response further. "Yes to the first part of knowing what it is that has you all edgy and no to the part of you telling me to get the fuck out yo' face."

"And the last statement I made was not 'get the fuck out of my face' but 'get the hell out of my face'."

Amused by her own remark, Nard caught a glimpse of her smile and continued to communicate.

"So there is a soft spot in that all-steel outfit you're wearin'."

Her seriousness portrayed earlier presented itself immediately.

"Haven't I told you that my man had to run a quick errand to handle some business and that he will be back?"

"No. But it gives me less than a little while to leave you feeling more pleased about my presence than when I first walked up on you."

Her menacing stare searched his eyes for the slightest sign of foolishness he might've spoken. She broke their trance and focused elsewhere.

"He always do this shit," she said aloud to herself.

"You mean your husband," he said, noticing her frustration.

"Yes! Every time he takes me out to have fun, some bullshit always pop up." She stared at him, stating, "The problem has started to become an every-event thing lately with us."

"I'm startin' to feel yo' pain, but then again I'm not."

"And what's that supposed to mean?"

"Lookin' in your eyes, a brotha' can see the hurt, and that since I'm not wearing any lady shoes, it's more of a woman-type thang with lil' input I can inform you on except to see it my way and let's do this the highway."

His smile joined by hers.

"And for what reasons?"

"Well, for starters, me being on some leaving you all out in the open on your own like I just met you would be unheard of." She continued listening in on his dialogue. "To top it off, not only will your forbidden space be preoccupied by mines, but every word that I speak," he shortened their distance, "would be so up and close that," his face came inches away from hers, "you would easily be able to chew one…letter…at…a…time…"

She made an effort at replying, but was speechless. His words managed to soften her heart. A second attempt at responding stumbled out of her mouth.

"Th-they call me Peaches."

"Peaches-n-crème," he said, stepping back a couple of feet. "My, my, my, the two perfect mixtures on a hot summer day. Oh, yeah, around the way, I'm known as Nard."

"Well, Nard, if you feel like your time is up, I'll understand."

Viewing his watch, he said, "Only if you feel my presence is no longer needed, it's cool with me."

"Have not you forgotten about my husband?" she asked, sounding unsure of her position.

"You know what, I was just about to ask you the same thang." Her admiration towards him displayed itself across her face. "I wouldn't do that if I was you. Your husband might not appreciate it."

CHAPTER: 13

Tosha accumulated a sweat in her short time of dancing. She snatched a handful of napkins off a couple's table en route to her friends' location and wiped her forehead dry. A waitress several tables over noticed the fingers Tosha held up for three club drinks. She swiped a drink toted by another waitress that passed her seat. Her friends watched as she hurriedly moistened her dry throat. The bitter, salty taste made her frown.

"Buuuuurp!"

"You triflin', girl."

"And you some shit. So I guess that makes us even." Tosha extended her tongue out at Shenequa. "How 'bout we take a good look around us and savor this moment of being surround by some of the world's finest men under our noses tonight, awaiting for me to give them the, 'go 'head baby…do you to me'!"

Meka informed, "Make sure what you don't do is scare them away running home to their mothers."

"I know that's right," laughed Shenequa.

"Could somebody please tell me why is the world filled with so many," Tosha pointed at Shenequa, "SHE-HATERS!"

Meka interrupted, "Either the man she's with is blind or life is like a box of chocolates cause the kid out there on the floor doesn't know what in the hell he got."

"And you wonder why I come between couples that are preoccupied. Just look at that thang' they call Miss Chicken Coop," commented Tosha.

"Now that one I can agree with you on. Girlfriend is in need of a touch-up, a turn-around and a touchdown," added Shenequa.

"Hold up. Hooold up, ladies!" Meka's tone shifted into a mode of seriousness. "But, my eyes have beamed in on, accidentally, a rather handsome young man that's well known to us all."

"Who?! Who?! Where?! Where's he at, girl?! Show me!"

Tosha's neck extended upward in search of the individual Meka referred to.

"I...be...god...damned!"

Shenequa became angered at what danced in the arms of another woman.

"Shenequa, calm down, girl. All the boy is doing is having a lil' fun."

Meka watched the frustration on her friend's face intensify. She tried placing a hand on Shenequa's shoulder, but it was swung off.

"What you tryin' to do, Meka? Save him from the beat down he's about to receive with his sassy ass? Just look at him."

"Y'all talkin' bout Mike out there? Negro, please! Here I am about to break my neck in search of someone fine as hell, only to notice her man, Mike. The midget."

"Talk to her, Tosha," pleaded Meka.

"Shenequa," she said, placing an arm around her neck. "I have only one thang to say to you. Handle...yo'...business!"

She stood up, knocking over her chair.

"Don't mind if I do."

Her path cleared of anyone possibly in her way.

"Why you tell that girl that, Tosha?"

"Cause...she's half of me and all of her."

"You have to excuse me for being so rude, but why in the hell would anyone want to leave you, out of all people, alone?"

"I don't know. I guess he feels his business is more pleasing than this," she said, brushing her hand down the outskirts of her protruding hips.

"I guess so," agreed Nard, staring at her curves. His perplexity disallowed him to understand her husband's actions. "You mind if I ask a question?" Their togetherness located in seclusion at the base of a darkened corridor that led to a private area of the club. He eventually was able to convince her in having a drink. She requested in socializing out of the sight of everyone. Her back pressed to the wall and arms folded, displaying comfort in his presence. He placed his palm beside her head on the wall for balance while standing in front of her. "Can you handle the truth?"

"Depends on what it is," she said, viewing his hand reach for hers.

He thought of moving himself completely against her body, but cautiously checked the area for any passersby. Their location provided him a minimum sight of the dance floor and Mike in rejoice with Carmen.

CHAPTER: 14

Shenequa hid herself in the midst of dancers. Mike's vulgar performance baffled her mind beyond comprehension. His behavior extended itself out of character at times, but far from what she witnessed tonight. Her head ducked low, hoping she would remain unseen. She crept, just shy of his location. By now, he faced opposite of his partner. Along his hips, she held to and pressed herself against him. Shenequa's contempt influenced her mind in performing an act of violence. Her foot flinched in an attempt to move faster. She wanted desperately to separate their togetherness. Instead, she humbled herself and stepped behind them. The steam blowing out of her nose onto Carmen's neck stiffened her movement. Fear flashed in her eyes at the sight of Shenequa standing over her shoulder.

"He's my man," whispered Shenequa in her ear.

Carmen abidingly eased herself off to a different area. Mike's ludicrous act continued, unaware of the change in women. She squeezed his booty.

"Haaay, shawty," he yelled. "We feelin' kind of lucky back there, ain't we!"

Her grasp intensified his excitement. His upper chest bent slightly downward in a swinging motion, repetitively. Still, her presence stood unknown. His exhaustion forced a stoppage. "That's it fo' me, shawty! I gots to take me a seat." He turned around and stared wide-eyed at her face. "SHENE—" but he felt the strength of her first plant itself over his eye.

The crowd cleared his fall. He tumbled to the floor in shame. She drug him by his collar back to the table. Tosha handed him a piece of ice out of her glass to help prevent any major swelling. Shenequa stepped off, returning with an ice pack. His face flopped on top of it in his hand.

Mike sensed the whispers at the table were about him, and lifted the unshielded eyelid to face his adversaries. Shenequa's hand rubbed across his wavy hair, signifying her continuing love. Her friends watched on in silence. Tosha began pounding her hand on the table while laughing out loud. Meka tried concealing her humor, but eventually gave in. His slouching posture sat upward. He removed the pack and searched Shenequa's face for answers.

"Why you do that?"

"You my man, and I can."

"Now my face all swollen up."

Nard caught sight of the entire scenario. He politely excused himself to assist his friend. His laughing finished way before he made it over to their area. Mike spun around to the hand he felt on his shoulder.

"Is this how those two lovebird friends of mines show their true feelings to the world?"

"This ain't funny, playboy."

"You damn right," retorted Shenequa. "That's why I punched you! And you better be glad I didn't start kicking you up and down yo' narrow ass."

"Does it hurt, daddy?" teased Tosha.

"You're very fortunately I can only see half of that Esther-ugly looking face of yours cause it would definitely be around two of what I just went through you keep running that lip."

"Don't worry, Mike," said Meka, "cause from the looks of things, Miss Shenequa wears the pants around here."

Shontae's presence standing beside Nard quieted his company. Mike grabbed ahold of Nard's wrist, informing him not to wonder off too far.

"Well, damn," contested Tosha at Nard's failure in introducing his friend, "ain't you rude!"

"Not as half as rude by keeping this young lady's identity confidential. Excuse us for a second, everyone."

He led her by the hand off to the side.

"I knew maybe one or two of them was pastime, Nard, but a whole table of them at one time, well, you are the man."

"Those are just some close friends of mine. The one holding the ice pack is my partna', Mike. Along with his lady giving him some assistance. The other two are just some foolish kids bumming for whatever they can get they hands on."

"You really didn't have to leave them, you know. I was just showing my respect by letting you know that not only have I seen you at the table, but also with another lady you was with before you went to the table."

His halfhearted mirth wasn't enough to convince her otherwise.

"So all that tells me then is that you haven't seen nuthin' but friendly conversation."

"If you want to call face to face with no space friendly, I'd hate to see the scene of you trying to be even friendlier."

"You're too much. You know that, right? Maybe that's why I dig you so much."

"You can't really mean that, do you?"

"And why not?"

"'Cause in order to get with this and I do mean this, you'll have to be dead serious, and from what I've seen, you're all games."

"So what you're saying is that if I unplug it and place all my chips back in my pockets, my life with you will be on easy streak?"

"No! All I'm sayin' is you do your thing and whenever you find the precious time to grow up...call me."

"YO! WHERE YOU—" He watched her walk off.

Peaches barely dodged Shontae's arm, heading in the direction of Nard.

"Could you please give me a ride the hell out of here, Nard? Anywhere!"

He searched past her and watched Shontae stare at him with discouragement. His mouth fixed itself to speak but observed her further their distance. Peaches blocked his sight entirely.

"Did you hear me, Nard?"

"Yeah, I heard you! What's up with hubby?"

"Are you afraid? If so, I can find someone else willing to take me."

"Me, afraid? Be serious, shawty. But give me a second to make sure my partna' straight."

She trailed him over to his friends. Shenequa continued catering to Mike's pain. He removed the eye pack, mouthing the words at Nard, "I warned you," and received a dismissive gesture in return.

"Everyone, this here is Peaches." She shared a wave. Tosha frowned, bewildered. "I'm about to drop shawty off, Mike. You aiight?"

"I'm straight. We'll hook up on a later date and time."

"By the way, playa', try to be on better point for that right hook, you feel me."

"Thanks for having my back, sir. Waaaay back," he said, bumping fists with Nard. "Well, ladies, aren't we ready to do the right thang, like get me the hell up out of here before the whole damn club knows who Mike is?"

"Boy, you gots to be crazy," uttered Tosha.

"I think it is time we left, ladies, so I can get my boo to the crib and tuck his butt into bed."

"You the driver," concurred Meka.

"Make his ass catch the cab or something," objected Tosha. "We just got here. Damn!"

CHAPTER: 15

Nard's thoughts drifted into bliss, envisioning him and Peaches laid out together on a sandy beach in the Bahamas, fiddling with one another's toes. She scooped a handful of sand and dumped it down his shorts. He stumbled to his feet and gave chase. His eyes temporarily ensnared on her flawless derriere, bouncing to a perfect rhythm. The thong she wore squeezed her vagina tighter in between the more her legs stretched apart, exposing its plumpness. Their fun came to an end, witnessing her stumble to the ground near the banks of shallow water caused by his diving grasp around her ankle. He kissed her on the feet. Calves. Thighs…

"If you aren't careful, we going to hit something."

"Huh? Say what?" He heard the last couple of words she stated, securing a firmer grip on the steering wheel. "Oh, yeah. Sorry 'bout that. My mind had wandered off."

"On?"

"You. Who else?"

"Your walk to the car seemed sort of nervous. I mean, you didn't have to do this if you didn't want to. It's not like I put a gun to your head or something."

"It wasn't so much as me being nervous, but let's be real here. You and I both know that we're treading in the danger zone and that there's no need of us being both foolish and careless."

"But sneaky, right?"

"Not sneaky, freely. You know, two adults come and go as they please. Not turning it in so early. Enjoying what's left of the night."

"Unless you have something wonderful stored in that head of yours, a sister is all ears."

Her ear moved toward him, awaiting any suggestions.

"I'm glad to see you are finally at ease with yo'self."

"Not really. But why bother you with the bs I'm dealing with in my life?"

"You're exactly right, cause I'd hate to leave such a fine ass lady on the side of the road bagging up traffic, tryn' to get a ride from every weirdo to psycho."

"You wouldn't do po' lil' Peaches like that, now, would you?"

"Peaches, pears, plums, whoever."

"You know, I still haven't forgotten about the truth or dare question that we left unfinished back at the club."

"I see we added a dare tactic along with the truth."

"Why not? A lil' dare-devilish never hurt anyone. Especially not this one."

"Is that so? Well, here's a dare-scare for ya." His mind juggled on a small proposition that wasn't too absurd. "I dare you, Peaches, to rub a finger or two between the split that's exposing your cleavage so elegantly."

"Is that all?"

He nodded yes. She let the upper part of her seat back a couple of notches, preparing a presentation. On a single hand, she seductively licked the inner part of her two longest fingers at the tips. Their spreading sloped softly and slowly over her partially exposed breast, coming to a halt at the area her bra pressed them together the tightest. He glimpsed back and forth, refusing to miss out on any part of her show. She ran her fingers across her flesh several times, which caused her nipples to harden through her shirt. Her full hand intervened in the act and began making circular motions on her entire chest. "Like that?" She planted her tongue on a breast lifted to her mouth, finishing off the performance.

"Exactly like that."

"My turn!" She pondered a task for him, then said, "I dare you, Nard, to take your right hand and massage my inner thighs."

Without hesitation, she placed his hand on her lap. She rested hers atop of his, directing it in a way she felt more appropriate. Gentle motions of up and down rubbing were steadily practiced on her legs.

"Are you feeling me yet?" Low sounds of moans clarified his answers. "At the rate we going, if a brotha' don't hurry up and find somewhere to continue our challenges, yours is gonna be over before mine even gets started."

"Hotel…motel…Holiday Inn…my treat!"

"'Nuff said."

CHAPTER: 16

Mike overheard Slim's and T-Funk's voices through the commotion up ahead upon his exit of the club. He hurriedly searched for another escape route in hopes of being unseen. His passaged steered him in one direction with no chance of eluding them. The ice pack held to his face fell to the floor. He planted the swelling deep in Shenequa's chest and glued his body to her side.

"EVERYBODY!" shouted Tosha. "THIS HERE IS MIKE! AND NOT ONLY DID MIKE JUST GOT BEAT UP BUT HE'S ALSO TRYIN' TO HIDE HIS FACE FROM PUBLIC VIEWING!"

He paused in midsentence of her statement. Tosha fought back his hands that were inches away from squeezing her neck. Shenequa withheld him long enough for his anger to subside. T-Funk eyed up ahead at a small group of people, hearing someone mention Mike's name.

"Ain't that…ain't that Mike up there? Don't his eye somewhat look kind of swollen?" Slim studied the male figure fitting Mike's description. "Let's see what the business is."

Without delay, they rushed through the crowd to his side, wanting to resolve any matters that might've occurred.

"Damn, peeps," stated T-Funk, "what's up? You got into some drama! Let's go handle this shit."

"He got into some drama, aiight," affirmed Shenequa. "From being socked in the eye by me and with me picking his ass up off the floor."

Slim's mind refused to accept what she had informed him of. He faced T-Funk and clearly understood the confusion expressed on his face as well. Slim drew the conclusion that Mike's prior mistakes had finally pressed Shenequa's buttons beyond the limit. Mike's irk converted to frustration, hearing his friends share their laughs.

"So now I'm the crowd clown. That's aiight. Gone and get yo' jokes off."

"Shit, playa'," spoke Slim. "You gots to be on point fo' that type of beef."

T-Funk added, "They say the percentage of a man being beaten by a woman is at an all-time high. Welcome to the adding statistics of number fo' hundred thousand and one."

Tosha's intriguing sight of T-Funk forced her body to position itself directly in front of his.

"Excuse me, brotha', but are you single and free to be with me?"

His friends patiently awaited a response.

"What's a' matter, Funk? Cat snatched yo' tongue?" joshed Slim.

"Sorry, cutie, but I'm married…with children!"

"If that's the case, why in the hell ain't you at home?" She studied his fingers in search of any female ties. "And where is your wedding ring?"

"You see, umm, today it had to be cleaned and I get it back in a couple of days."

"And I'm supposed to believe that three seconds and counting ass lie of yours too?"

"Yep. And as for you, Mike, the only thing I can tell you is to lay low, cater to the swelling, and holla' back at a pimp when you're one hundred percent."

"Will do. Now y'all two gone and finish off the night inside with a bang for me. It's just too bad my bang finished me off completely."

"That's okay, baby," intervened Shenequa, placing a kiss on his lips. "Love always hurts, they tell me."

As the night lingered on, setting the foundation for lovers to mingle, two individuals calmly laid on top of one another in a world of disinfectant and clean sheets. His broad, flawless chest seeping through the dim light painted a silhouette on the wall. She removed her hands away from his pecs and rubbed them down his lower back, descending into complete darkness. The top half of his body arched itself upward. His hands planted underneath her armpits. Her succulent breasts adored his technique of nibbling on her nipples. Their movements came to a cease. Her eyes pierced through his in hopes of finding answers to the questions asked in her private thoughts.

"As for the part of you handling the truth, to have you in the arms of this brotha' is a black man's heaven come true. It's just too bad yo' husband is tryin' to turn you into a black woman hell."

She angled her head off to the side, letting a slight sign of depression structure her beauty. He placed a finger at the base of her chin and guided her face in the direction of his.

"Must you remind me, Nard?"

"No, no, nothin' like that. But it's obvious you're not happy because as the two of us lay here with you waiting for me to explore your deepest and most inner being, it's only right that your attention is focused on me and me only."

"What more can I do to show you?"

"First, you could start by allowing me to guide your body to a more suitable position." She nudged him on the side, signaling to lay on his back. "Perfect. Next, I would like to lay here and witness Peaches kiss me here. Kiss me there. Anywhere you feel is appropriate."

He closed his eyes, feeling her mouth smother his. Their passionate moment forced an instant erection that caused his stiffness to press itself against her vagina. Her tongue departed out of his ear and slid onto his neck, chin, and further down his chest. She stopped right above his navel.

"Has anyone ever told you that your navel is cute?"

"Has anyone ever told you you're making me weak as hell?"

"Will there be any more controlling of the mind, sir?"

"Politely, and gently, stroke my manhood until you hear it moan."

"Until it what?"

"You know, reaches its fullest length and is ready for you."

She slid herself just above his midsection and took hold of his penis. Her hand stroked him with a delicate touch of precision. His eyes rolled around in his head, strongly attracted to the softness of her palms.

"How is that?"

Opening an eyelid, he said, "Shawty, I couldn't have done it any better."

"Are you finally convinced that all my attention is focused on you only?"

"My job is to make sure your head is clear of all nonsense so you can be fully aware of our sexual encounter."

She placed a finger over his lips, quieting him. Her frame moved backwards and rested on top of his phallus. He could feel the moistness between her legs, grinding slowly where she craved for him the most. Unable to wait, her lower body lifted upward and clamped ahold of his erection at the base of her opening. She gradually eased her body downward, cherishing every inch that slowly made its way deeper inside of her.

"Hold up a second, Peaches. I think we might need to place something down there between us."

He grabbed a latex from underneath his pillow that he'd placed there before she'd laid down in bed with him. She removed it from out of his possession, split the package, and shielded him. Her nails clawed into his chest as she lowered herself back to their starting position.

CHAPTER: 17

"It's over, Fancy."

"What do you mean, it's over?! Who the hell are you to just cut off our affair cold turkey like that, negro? No, sir! No way! You done bumped yo' damn head! You promised me long ago that you and Peaches were startin' to lose love for one another. That dick belongs to me now, mister. So go on and get out of the car and show mommy some of that big daddy love she needs in her life." He pressed the button that kept her from snatching open the door she pulled on. "Get out the damn car, D-Man! Don't make me beg for what's rightfully mine!"

He sometimes questioned himself as to why he'd laid down with a stripper in the first place. The rules posted above the door of his former office to Pink Plush Strip Club clearly stated: "The first taste is a mistake, the second lick means you're weak!" Words he lived by, even long after quitting the business. Fancy was a sight any man would find hard to resist. To him, she was drop-dead gorgeous. Her one-hundred and fifty pound frame fitted itself extremely well inside her five-foot, six inch height. Sleek hair extended to the middle area of her back. Not a single flaw was noticeable on her hourglass figure. In her short span as an employee, her demeanor had boasted itself in a professional manner. The majority of the spectators were convinced she'd been in her line of work for years. His experience gave him the advantage in recognizing a new jack from a veteran, and he knew without guessing that she was fresh meat.

Fancy watched him through the slit of curtains on stage, seated in his private area the night she deceived him. He preoccupied most of his time studying the screen to his laptop he toted around. She figured he wasn't so much interested in the women and kept busy with his business. They conversed on several occasions without him ever requesting of her precious time or body. D-Man admired her intelligence, but kept her at a distance. Her minor background investigation of him revealed his status as a major narcotics distributor. She wasn't the least bit enthused by his reputation, nor money. Her main concern was having him between her legs the more he tried ignoring her.

The suction he felt on his neck caught him off guard. Her hands slid across his chest as she stepped out of the darkness from behind his chair. She sat on his lap. He allowed her childish game to play itself out, or until she knew he wasn't the least bit interested.

"So you're the man everyone brags about."

"Any problems?"

"Not at all, sir."

"So why are you sitting in mine?"

"Cause yours roomier than a chair. Bigger to adjust myself with," she said, squirming her waist around in a circle.

"Oh, really?"

"You can't feel it enlarging itself?"

He hadn't denied her truth. His temptation against resisting her was worsening. She leaned her mouth to his ear, whispering, "Big Daddy...you can have all of this...for a lil' bit of," she clutched his dick, "that."

Her tongue penetrated deep inside his earlobe. It circled outwards and down the side of his cheekbone. She gripped him tightly at the chin, forcing his lips to meet hers. D-Man sat motionless in compliance of her behavior.

She separated from his mouth, speaking in his ear, "Big Daddy, I perform even better when you're laid out flat on your stomach."

He later moved her into a condo and demanded that she quit her job. The affair lasted for six months before he decided it was best if he cut all ties with her. For the past month, he contemplated on the right time to inform her. Tonight presented the opportunity. His convincing stare into her eyes numbed the center core of her heart entirely.

"I'm finished, Fancy, and I mean that."

Tears were streaming down her face, and they bounced off the side of his car. The silent moan to his Cadillac engine awakening caused her to act frantically.

"Don't do this, daddy," she said, holding on to the slow-moving vehicle. "Please don't do this." She ran along the side of the car until his speed increased. "I HATE YOU, NIGGA!" Her thrown purse landed on the back of the windshield, scattering her belongings over the street.

He returned to the club in desperate search of his wife. Halfway in, someone stood shaking his hand uncontrollably to turn and identify two huge front teeth. Shawty Jack, the club owner, almost shook loose D-Man's arm. Repeated thanks for his help for the place's success were shouted over and over again in his ear, somewhat starting to irritate him. He spotted J-Dub a short distance off. Shawty Jack watched D-Man depart without having said a single word.

"You seen Peaches?"

J-Dub glanced over his shoulder.

"D-Man! What's up, homeboy?"

"I said, have you seen Peaches?"

"Nah, homeboy." D-Man scanned the entire room for her, to no avail. "You know what, D-Man, now that you mention it, she was with some young cat not too long ago, headed out the front door."

"Boy, look here. You betta' not be shittin' me with some bs, tryin' to put me in my feelings for what I did to yo' sorry ass partna' earlier today."

"Come on, man! That incident was between y'all two. You felt it needed to go there, well, that's on you. And what I look like, playin' with you about yo' main squeeze anyway? I know you mean business. But she did walk out, and that's on everything I love."

His temper surged when he was unable to identify her anywhere.

"J-Dub...see you payday."

"Hopefully you won't look down on me after what went on tonight," she said, straightening herself out in the mirror.

"Come here and let me explain something to you." He patted a spot on the bed for her to take a seat next to him. "What you did tonight, any female in a stressful predicament such as yours would've done the same. If not worse."

"You think so?"

"I know so. I'm just thankful it was me you decided to open yo'self up to."

"I bet you are, silly."

"But seriously though, I want you to think about where you see yourself in the next five years and see if it comes anywhere close to where you are now." Her attention blankly averted towards the floor. "One thang I'm not tryin' to do and that's get you to leave yo' man. But you need to ask yourself, are you really where you wanna be?"

"One day, whenever you decide to marry, you're gonna make some woman real proud of you."

"And why is that?"

"You're a very forward person. Sincere-like in your words."

"I do my best."

"Will I ever see you again?" she asked, preparing her departure.

"Remember this. 777-9311. Use that when you're in need of some serious comfort."

"Take care of yourself, Nard."

"Sho'nuff. You do the same."

Her waving hand faded away behind the closing door.

CHAPTER: 18

Peaches' scenic route while traveling in the backseat of a taxi gave her a sense of freedom. Enough time to convince herself that a change for the better would be coming. Soon. Away from the crime-infested life of her husband. Quality time with someone who was more concerned for her than life itself. Similar to when she and D-Man were inseparable during the early stages of their relationship.

The coldness of her fears forced a shiver through her lost soul. Her escort busied himself with directions, never once noticing her sorrow. A harsh, southern farm accent echoed throughout the ride and came to a halt in front of her driveway.

"Miss, that'll be fifteen dollas', ya' hear." His meaty hand reached over the seat, accepting her money. She shut the door and stared up at her darkened residence.

"MISS!" he shouted out of the passenger window. "I said fifteen dollas', not fifty dollas', ya hear!"

"Yes, I hear you. Just consider it a gift of reason. Goodbye."

Familiar sounds to "Love Don't Cost A Thing" were playing out of their bedroom on her way up the stairs. D-Man was lounged at the foot of his bed, watching her enter. Her walk slowed itself almost to a completed halt as she studied his stillness inside the dim room. His path had to be cleared in order for her to make it into the bathroom. Her pace eventually picked itself back up.

"I see you made it home safely."

She turned the door handle with caution and felt his strength squeezing her grip.

"Ouch, D-Man!"

"Hold up a minute before you go in there. Seeing that it's, like, twenty-five minutes after 2 a.m., I thought you might've forgotten your way home."

"Could you please let go?"

"How did you leave the club tonight?" he asked, releasing her.

"By cab."

"By cab all the way home, or halfway home?"

"What difference does it make?"

She landed in the opposite direction of her Gucci pouch on the floor from his hardened slap.

"That's what difference it makes. And along with the gentleman who politely escorted you out the door, too."

She slid herself back into a corner of the room, trying to avoid any further contact. He bent down on his knees beside her and reached out his hand.

"Don't touch me!"

"I'm only trying to get an understanding, baby. That's all."

"What do you want from me?" she sobbed in fear.

"To make sure my wife is aiight. Is that asking too much?"

"Please...just get away from me."

"That's how you playin' it? Ok then. Have it your way." In disbelief, she watched him unzip his slacks. "Remember that problem I was having earlier?" He slid is pants down. "It's just been cured." She tried crawling away, feeling him tug at her ankle. "Not so fast, young lady."

She heard the sound of clothes tearing as she attempted to free herself.

"Stop! You bastard! Let me go!"

She managed to wriggle herself out of his grasp and jumped to her feet, sprinting through the bedroom door.

"You right. Get the fuck out of here before I change my mind."

Chapter: 19

"Will you be staying or leaving, sir?"

Nard's head shifted around on the pillow, pressing it down harder. The repeated words in his slumber vibrated his mind awake. Dangling sounds of keys outside the door forced his head to raise up. A maid entered the room in tow of cleaning supplies. His presence frightened her.

"Oh, I'm sorry, sir." She pressed a hand against her pounding chest. "I knocked on the door and yelled inside several times. I figured no one was in here."

His face plopped down in the pillow as he mumbled, "No problem, and nah, I'm on my way out in just a minute."

She took a second peep at his frame in a pair of boxers, stretched out on the bed. He eventually got up, scrounging for his clothes, which were laid throughout the room. A bathroom rag soaked in steamy hot water washed away any sleep possibly left in his eyes. He checked the room for more of his belongings and then embraced a heavy whiff of fresh air upon opening the door.

The room key was handed over at the front desk. Sunday morning commuters of God worshippers flooded the streets, blending him in traffic. He reached for his cellphone, stationed in the passenger seat, dialing Mike's number. Several rings surpasses before the word "Hello" intercepted.

"If it ain't the queen of the ring." Shenequa held his ear captive, declaring her reason for battery. "Yeah, yeah. I know, I know. You could've at least given him a body shot or somethin'. Anythin' besides a blow to the dome. What about the swellin'? It went down some, right? Somewhat? Good. When he wakes up, tell him I said to give me a holla'. Peace."

The chiming sound of his Blackberry alerted him to an unfamiliar number displayed across its screen. He ignored it for as long as he could and pressed a button. The hostility detected in a woman's voice wasn't the tone he was expecting this early in the day.

"Who is this? Peaches! Calm down, shawty…calm…down. Now, start over again, but this time say it slower." The pain detected in her voice subsided long enough for him to listen. "Let me get this straight. You said that your husband slapped you? For what?" His head rested against the window, vexed at her ongoing dialogue. "Where you at now? The Waffle House? On the north side? I'm on my way." He tossed his phone on the seat. "What in the hell have you gotten yourself into this time, homeboy?"

Less than thirty minutes elapsed before he pulled into the parking lot. In and out, customers politely excused themselves as they passed him standing glued to the entrance door. The thought of walking back to his car and acting as if she never existed seemed the best choice. Though he was the actual cause to her problem, his pride wouldn't dare tolerate him evading another one of life's minor obstacles he initiated.

Off to the far corner, she sat, unaware of his arrival. Her trance continued, veering through the window behind a pair of Dolce and Gabana shades, refusing to acknowledge the commotion that surrounded her. He ordered two glasses of orange juice and tip-toed in her direction.

"Hi. Are we alone?" He extended her a glass.

"Not anymore," she said, accepting his generosity.

"Would you mind bringing that gorgeous face of yours close to mine so I can examine what you're partially covering up?" He sat across from her and placed his elbows on top of the table. He removed her shades. "So this is the work of Mr. I-The-Wed."

"It hurts, too, Nard."

He leaned inward, brushing a finger over the outskirts of its swelling.

"Is that better?"

"Much better. Thank you for coming on such short notice. I know you said to call you when in need of some comfort, so what time would be better than now?"

"Don't even trip, shawty. Have you had enough time to decide on what you gonna do yet?"

"Not really. Maybe I'll go live with my mother for a while. She's about the only relative I have close by until I find my own place."

"Financially wise. You aiight then?"

"Oh, definitely. Don't get it twisted. The boy is loaded with money and I did have enough sense to open my own savings account with the funds he was giving me for hard times whenever they might occur."

"Now, run down the whole ordeal for me."

"Well," she said, releasing a sigh, "I walked in the room. He was sitting up waiting for me. Asked me how I got home. Then," she built up her strength to finish the sentence, "he backhanded me."

"Just like that."

"And then…"

"Damn! There's more?"

Her voice started trembling. Her eyes swelled with tears.

"He…he…tried to…he tried to rape me, Nard."

She watched him stand and slide next to her on the wooden bench. His arm stationed itself around her for comfort.

"All because of me."

"Why would you say that?" She ceased her weeping.

"Cause I shouldn't have been invading on yo' husband's privacy."

"It's more my fault than anything. Especially after leaving the club, not knowing who in the hell might've seen us. All of this could've easily been avoided if I would've just told you to get the fuck out of my face instead of get the hell out of my face."

Traces of a grin slightly carved her lips.

"You right, now that you mention it."

"But all the bs he was leaving me to deal with just made me blank out all thoughts of him. I'm only human with needs that aren't too much to ask of."

"I'm kind'a shook up about yo' man tryin' to play you as the role of a stripper. Particularly one who was almost forced to participate in disagreement."

"Thank God he didn't." The weight of her head rested on his shoulder. "What am I gonna do now, Nard?"

Silence accompanied them for a brief moment.

"First of all, you gotta have a policeman escort you to his crib to get all of your possessions. Then, take it from there."

"One day at a time."

"As for me, my ass betta' be a helluva' lot careful 'bout being with no married woman again if this is gonna be the outcome."

"That mouthpiece of yours is very contagious to a woman who is being neglected by a person they're supposed to be in love with."

"Everything happens for a reason. Now I gotta make sure yo' man don't come for no revenge, wanting to do me in."

Her head lifted, facing his. "I doubt it. He probably was waiting for something like this to happen just so he could get rid of me."

"As pretty as you arc? SHIIIIT! Me looking for the man who manipulated my wife would no doubt be at the top of my list."

"Don't worry, Nard. I got your back."

"I appreciate that. You need a ride or anything?"

"I'm alright. I plan on calling a cab as soon as I can unglue myself from this seat."

"Well," he said, rising to his feet, "make sure you contact me when you get situated."

"Okay. And Nard…"

"Yeah."

"Be careful."

CHAPTER: 20

Record highs of summer heat continued to blister the city pavement. The Ramada Inn sprinkler system kept its even-cut lawn in a miraculous state. A landscaping crew busied themselves working on the immaculate hedges surrounding its perimeter. The pollen blown into the air irritated Nard's allergies during his short walk to room 112. He arose around 7 a.m., craving pecan waffles and a side dish of scrambled eggs. Charlene had slept the entire time, unaware of his departure. She laid stationary in the same position he'd left her when he entered.

The shuffling of papers brought her pretty face out from underneath the covers. She slid next to him on the bed, rubbing his solid abdomen. He paused to question her behavior, but diverted his sight at what flashed across the Sansui flat screen.

Naked, she rose off of the bed and blocked his view. He froze. She pranced up to him and rested her D-sized breasts in front of his face. He placed the food down. She lifted his shirt off. Their mingling converted to intercourse. His cell phone rang. She held his wrist back and proceeded straddling. It rang again. The intense shivering of her body allowed him to free his wrist. An extreme outflow of her juices forced her to collapse on his chest.

His body swung itself upright at the sound of Peaches' voice. Charlene landed off to the side of him. Her attitude broadcasted severe disdain that he wasn't concerned with. She wrapped an arm around his in hopes of him ending the negligence he displayed. He ended the phone dialogue and snatched his arm free.

"Is this what they mean by 'you got it made'?"

"I'm off the phone and you're still not happy. I'm sayin', shawty." He reclined under the sheets. "If you hatin', let me know, cause this playa' can easily escort you out the front door."

"Damn! Must we be so all uptight about it?"

"My fault, shawty. It's just that a brotha' is still feeling a lil' incomplete for this enjoyable morning of ours. How about completing the other half off with some orange juice, if you catch my drift."

His head motioned towards the area between his legs, which was protruding through the sheets.

"My favorite. Breakfast in bed." She was enthused at his offer. "If you continue to spoil me like this, I might not want to let you leave my sight. For good!"

Her head faded out of sight, embracing his problem.

"YO! PEACHES! WHAT'S HAPPENIN'!"

His shouting reminded her just how much she still resented him. She'd manage to evade him since their last encounter. Her hate was strong, but not enough to involve the constable. Their assistance was requested in escorting her in and out of his premises to gather her belongings. She was furious he'd bumped into her today at the mall. Her stride kept its pace without the slightest sign of slowing down. He gave chase and positioned himself in front of her path.

"What's happening, you said? Me, about thirty seconds from calling the police on your black ass."

"That won't be necessary. I'm just trying to reconcile our differences for my foolish act that forced you to leave this man all alone and lonely." They stood in silence, their conversation intensifying. "I'm just tryin' to reconcile our differences for my foolish act that forced you to leave this man all alone and lonely. I never had the chance to really tell you the reason for what I did, which was to show you that I was dead serious about our marriage and that me doing what it looked like I was going to do was more of a scare tactic, which definitely wasn't gonna lead into me doing the unthinkable to you."

"What about you slapping me? I'd say your scare tactic turned into an all-out drill." He stepped closer. She moved back. He tried again and identified her fury. "You move any god-damn closer to me and I swear I'll yell so loud that you are trying to rape me, the mannequins will come alive and tackle that ass of yours down to the ground until the REAL people come to my rescue."

He blurted aloud, "What in the hell would you have done if you heard your husband left out the club with another woman?"

"I'd probably have left you. But certainly without any abuse."

"I love you, Peaches…and to hear that shit from someone under my wings about you and whoever he was had me messed up in the head."

"'Bout the same way I felt when you left me in the club. ALONE! And the bullshit that happened at your cookout too. Plus many others."

"All reasons was for business, baby."

"Did you ever think at all that your 'business' was coming between the best thing you ever had going on in your life?"

"That's why I stand here in front of you now. To try and straighten out our differences."

"We stand with my back towards you, with nothing more to say but to sign the divorce papers when you receive them."

"Ya-you kidding me, right?"

"The papers will be in the mail. Sooner than you think."

"What more is there for me to say?" he expressed with discouragement.

"BYE!"

Their hardened stares lasted for some odd seconds before he decided to bow down to her bravery.

"Make sure you tell whoever made all this possible to watch his ass."

"Don't even think about it."

He felt a gust of wind from her swift departure.

"Shontae," she said, patting her cousin on the arm, "look at that dress, girl."

"Where, child?"

"Over there. In the window of Macy's. The most beautiful damn dress I've ever seen."

Angel paused to observe the satin material. She glued herself to the window, fantasizing about how well it would rest across her plus-size figure. Or probably how her body inside it would halt any man that crossed her path.

"That is a luxurious item you're admiring."

"Yeah, well, it's just too damn bad my luxurious money is an indigent habit. As in, can't shop, won't shop. 'Bout the same as these brogans on my feet that's killing me. Need a new pair, but won't dare."

"Let me find out you got a stingy girl grip on your currency."

"If you was tryin' to hold on to what you got, living in a single-bedroom apartment along with attending college, that tail of yours wouldn't be so woopty-woop neither."

"I hear you. And feel you."

She managed to pull Angel away. Compared to when they first arrived during the morning, the mall capacity had increased tremendously. Kids were starting to run rampant out of stores, leaving behind signs of recklessness for employees to straighten out. Not a guardian in sight.

"Reminds me of the time when we was young and wild. Especially that time auntie spanked yo' butt inside a store that was flooded with customers." She dared believe Angel had stolen a soda and candy bar off a counter, devouring them without a care in the world. Her mother ran up behind out of nowhere, knocked the items out of her hand, and whipped her down a long isle until she was tired. "Yo' mother meant that beating that day."

"But what she didn't know was that I was dressed for the occasion with extra panties and jeans on. Hell, I got tired of waking up at night, wishing for a wish sandwich, as po' as we was."

"So you mean to tell me you had already planned for that event? Why, you sneaky lil' devil. No wonder you didn't cry that long. The way she swung her arm back and forth looked as if she was tryin' to kill someone."

"She was. Herself."

Angel arrived yesterday evening at her doorstep, luggage behind her. Spellman College had taken its two-week summer break. What better place, she thought, to relax herself than at her favorite cousin's place? Shontae gladly greeted her whenever she showed up, guestroom in complete preparation. She sometimes traveled to the campus, surprising Angel. One easily favored the other to an event of window shopping, and Shontae woke out of her sleep this morning, knowing the sole purpose of Angel's disturbance.

"You hungry, girl?"

Angel uttered, "Your treat or the restaurant's?"

Angel hinted of an illegal act she influenced Shontae to participate in when they were in high school. One they hadn't experienced in several years since exiting an all-night buffet without leaving a tip, nor for the amount of food they devoured.

"How 'bout our treat this time. You pay for mine and I'll pay for yours."

"Spoken like a true relative."

The common area withheld the noisiest commotion. Occupants stood shoulder to shoulder in loud shouts of whatever food was chosen at a variety of restaurants. A pizzeria handed the ladies several triangular boxes that were on display. They squeezed past awaiting customers and hurried off to a table out of harms way.

"This pizza looks good as hell," Shontae excitedly mentioned. "Pardon my French."

"Tell me where you see some kids at."

"Thank you for the reassurance, and I'll holla' back at you when I'm on the last bite of this pizza."

"I second that motion. Can't you hear my gut screaming for some type of attention?"

The unwrapping of paper, small bites, slurps out of straws, and light belches were the only sounds heard at their table.

"Pardon me, ladies."

Shontae raised her head.

"Yes. Can I help you somehow?"

The stranger heard resentment in Shontae's voice.

"But aren't you Shontae?"

"Yes, I am, and how would you know that?"

The woman stretched out her hand. Shontae just stared at it.

"My name is Peaches," pulling her hand back. "Anyway, Nard has told me so much about you in the short period of time I've known him."

"And?"

"And, he's a very wonderful man in so many ways imaginable that a woman could ever dream of."

"Would you please cut with the bullshit, miss?"

"Well, I just wanted to say, whatever it is you have done to make him mention your name so much has made things somewhat difficult for me. Well, for us."

Shontae sprung out of her seat and invaded the woman's space.

"Listen here…Miss…Peaches. Whenever I decide to really reel Mr. Nard in, believe me, it will bring no sweat from my legs or mouth."

Angel studied the scenario under close supervision. She decided it was best if she raised out of her seat.

"Well, Miss Shontae, one thing I can say about this young lady is that these doors from in between and what I speak with are always open for Nard at any time he gets ready."

"Bitch! You betta——"

Angel snatched her cousin back before she had a chance to land her hand across Peaches' face.

"Have a nice day, ladies."

The sarcasm in Peaches' voice drove Shontae hysterical. Angel still refused to turn her lose until Peaches was completely out of sight.

"Who was that?!" She released her cousin.

"Nobody. Just some chicken head that seems to be ahead of herself about Nard."

"And WHO is this Nard? Cause from the looks of it, I damn sho' can use me one."

"A young man who's been after me for over a few months. Well, since junior high school, to be exact."

"And why is Shontae making him chase her around?"

"He doesn't know how to keep his 'thang' in his pants, as you've just seen."

"Obviously, whoever he displays it to has one hell of a side effect, and I don't mean a bad one. I mean, have you ever sat down with the boy to talk to him about why he can't keep it zipped up in those baggy denims?"

"No. For one, he's too busy running from house to house, sponsoring g-string attire to women who are interested."

"Maybe it's time you clipped the string from around his waist so he'll have to stay in your home until further notice."

"That's easier said than done."

"When was the last time the two of y'all talked?"

"At the club a while back, when he wasn't so much trying to be up in Miss Poodle's face."

"The girl who just left?"

"You know it."

"You haven't tried to get in touch with him since then?"

"No, I haven't. He paged me once, earlier this week, but I didn't call back."

"Let me find out. Kenfolks don't know how to tame the savage beast."

"What's taking you so long?"

"Oh, trust me, when I set the trap for the ferocious one, his ass will be all paws with no claws, not knowing nothing else to do but sit, roll over, and fetch me."

"All in due time, I suppose."

"That's right. Time is the best thing on my side, cause we both can go fast or move slow. But what you need to do is whenever the next time you and Nard talk, dig off into his thought process to see what's clicking, and nothing more."

"Maybe you're right. At the rate Peaches is going, her goal is to make him lame."

"Leaving that poor man's world in a daze."

"Come on. Let's get out of here, girl."

CHAPTER: 21

2-Piece stumbled to the ground, blood trickling from his nose. He refused to accept that D-Man had declared war. A foot to his ribs landed him face-down in the dirt. He caught a glimpse of another incoming kick and barely dodged it. His quick reaction spun him around to a standing position. D-Man rushed him again, but stopped to watch his employee sprint for the woods that encircled the park. J-Dub yelled for him to wait up. His words went ignored. 2-Piece regretting not having carried his twins in their double-shoulder holsters to the cookout, and wanted very soon to right his wrong.

He hadn't been away from the scene of crime for more than an hour, praying his enemy hadn't left yet. Gun in one hand, the other in its holster. The wooded area and tall grass provided for him a perfect hiding location for his mission. Shooting skills acquired at a gun range in the past prepared him to hit his mark from up to 500 feet. His target was possibly less than 400, which made the task much easier. On one knee, he knelt, and searched for his comfort zone. The silencer was screwed in at the barrel's mouth. His right arm fully extended, supported by his left hand. He loosened his grip off of the handle, securing a firmer hold. The trigger finger found its rightful position. A clear aim of the back of the victim's head. D-Man sat on a bench, laughing. 2-Piece smiled, and slowly squeezed the trigger towards a click. In a split second, a little girl ran and jumped into D-Man's lap. His forefinger hesitated, and finally eased off the trigger. His eyes swelled as he watched on. Badly, he'd wanted D-Man dead, but decided on another day. Definitely another time.

J-Dub drove alongside the evening skies, uncertain of his friend's whereabouts. No one had seen, nor heard, from 2-Piece in over a month. Not since the altercation at the cookout. J-Dub's quest to find him was nearing its end. He wasn't sure whether to blame himself or not for failing to intervene in 2-Piece's and D-Man's altercation. A choice he would probably regret for the rest of his life. A chance at talking with his friend might not change the past, but it would at least clear up some of J-Dub's doubts that bothered him lately.

The apartment complex 2-Piece resided in was several blocks away. J-Dub couldn't pass up the chance of him possibly being at home, so he traveled in that direction. In the lot sat a violet-blue Escalade on 28 inch rims. It was the vehicle 2-Piece loved the most out of his five cars and trucks. He parked next to it and raced up the stairs to his apartment. He pounded on the thick, wooden door. He listened for any signs of movement on the inside.

"Open this damn door, fool! I know you're in there!" He knocked again. Still, no sound. "Don't make me kick this door down, playboy!"

His excitement subsided. Hopes of seeing 2-Piece started to fade. Down the steps he traveled.

"Da hell wrong with you, man? Banging on my door as if you were the feds or somebody. You 'bout to get your head blown off with that bullshit."

"What's up, playboy?" He raced back up. "Yo' boy been worried crazy 'bout you famm. Sho' yo' peeps some love." They briefly shared a strong embrace. "I been tryin' to get at you to see what's poppin' for the longest. After the incident at the park, it's like…you vanished off the face of the earth or something."

"Come on in and let me put you up on what's happenin'." Accumulated dust particles floated off the coffee table, where he'd grabbed a pack of cigarettes. They relaxed out on his couch. "Yo' man had to go and leave town to get my mind right first before I put this big boy plan into effect." He inhaled his cigarette.

"What plan? You plottin' without feelin' in home-team? That's how we roll now?"

"Nah, J. This plan had me taking a trip to chill with my two kids out of state, to let 'em know daddy is on his way home to live with them. For good!"

"What you sayin'?"

"Shit goes beyond what I'm sayin', but what's about to take place."

J-Dub identified the seriousness in his words and decided to change the topic over to a less intense one.

"What you eatin' on anyway in this ghost town place of yours, cause if you haven't," he said, spinning a blunt around in his hand, "I keep an appetite pleaser."

"Good lookin'." He lit it off his cigarette and laid the Newport 100 in the ashtray. "The man they call D-Man," he said, inhaling the smoke, "is like a tombstone away from his deathbed. Yeah! You heard right. To load my babies, aim—" exhaling through his nose, "and open fire on his ass anywhere I see fit."

"Code of the streets—"

"We play to keep leaving those who fake resting in peace."

"I'll break it down to you like this, you see…the shit he did was messed up and whatnot, and he could've handled it a better way. But if I would've tried to jump in, you know it would've turned into an all-out gun battle, except for you was slippin' anyway, and we was crazy outnumbered like hell. Not that it matters, but damn…some things we have to respect under certain conditions. Plus, to me, he didn't really get off on you like that anyway, to be honest."

"Just enough for me to decide it's la-la land for the big man."

"All the way to heaven, baby."

The effects of the marijuana slowed their words to silence. 2-Piece envisioned D-Man's blood on his hands. J-Dub's finger twirled the smoke around above his head.

"Every time I think about that sucka' duck, my hands reach for my two pieces. And damn a biscuit with a drank."

"Here," he said, squeezing a last pull off the shortened blunt before passing it. "Let this help you slow yo' roll before sparks start to appear out of somewhere unknown to the both of us."

"Oh, them babies is safe over there in their holsters, hanging up on the hat rack cocked and loaded."

"Any set date for the drama to start?"

"Let him continue to feel comfortable and relax, then let the unexpected turn into the unbelievable."

"Yo' plans for the finishing night?"

"Go and blow the continuing free money of D-Man's."

"I suppose there's no way I can talk you out of this one."

"Not this time, J baby."

"Just checkin', dogg."

"Certain shit I allow to skate, but this one…this one right here, will ride with me all the way to the end, you dig."

They stood up, arms spread to embrace one another. J-Dub headed towards the front door, and 2-Piece trailed him.

"I love you like a brotha', man. Always remember that. And if we never turn corners, burn blunts, or sex these shawties together again, a man's integrity is all there is in this world that he has to carry him. Keep it real, kenfolks."

"Don't go gettin' all soft on me, J. Yo' man just gotta do what he should've done a long time ago."

"Til' we ride again, then."

J-Dub signaled a peace sign to his longtime childhood friend, who watched him walk down the stairs. He closed the door and stretched out on his sofa. For so long, he and J-Dub had been tighter than a virgin's vagina. A friend couldn't possibly describe what one might've considered of the two. A bond of sacred trust and loyalty defined such a relationship. Killing wasn't so much the problem for 2-Piece, but leaving J-Dub to survive on his own was. He recited a prayer shortly after his eyelids had shut: "God has given man more than enough when He first gave us life! What lies in between it is the only important thing one must strive for while alive…sanity! Anything else is a lost cause. May our world unite again in the skies of heaven or beneath the surface of hell. One love, brotha'!"

CHAPTER: 22

"There's no place like home. I say, I saaaaid, there's noooo…place…
like…hooooooooome! Thank you! Thank you! Thank you very much!
Please, please, no autographs, no autographs!" Water bounced off of
his bare flesh in the shower. He was enjoying every moment of being
back in his home. The remodeling extended an extra week, which
meant further abuse and scolding inflicted by his mother. Pain he
refused to continue tolerating. He decided best to wait the remaining
days at a hotel. Ms. Hick tried convincing him back home, swearing
her behavior would change. "Are you serious, momma?" "Hell nah,
son! I thought it might sound good just sayin' it." Reacquainting
himself with a place he actually considered his own never felt better
to him.

The cleansing of his body lasted up to twenty minutes. He stepped
out, grabbing ahold of a towel off the rack, admiring his nudity in
a mirror. Shielded in his favorite, robe, he ventured towards the
kitchen. A loud knock at the front door detoured him. Two gentlemen
stood outside, and he could see them through the peephole. One was
excited, and the other was trying to settle him down.

"Aiight, gents. Could somebody tell me what the password is
before entering? And please, be sure you get it right."

"Let me think…is it…yours, mines, her body and time?"

"I couldn't have said it any better. Please," he said, sliding the
door ajar, "step right in to the Playa's Palace."

"What up, fool," said Mike, entering.

"What up, fool," repeated lil' man, stepping in behind his father.

"This, here," he said, placing a hand on his son's head, "is what the future ain't ready for. A new and improved me in its finest with three to the left, and right of him under his arms. All stallions!"

"Unc's house is like that, dad."

Historical portraits of African culture hung on his living room walls. New furniture still sealed in its plastic. Twin lamps displayed price tags, which held their cords in a knot on top of glass night stands on opposite ends next to the couch. A bubblegum machine was stationed in the far corner beside an ivory statue of a lion painted in gold.

"Yeah, you right. Unc' do got it going on. How 'bout it, Unc'? Feels good to be back where it's all at?"

"Mom-dukes had went a lil' overboard with the motherly love type thang."

"She wasn't trippin' like that I know."

"Was she! Things got so bad that I had to live in a hotel this past week. I couldn't continue taking that kind of abuse anymore. And she gave me a permanent scar on my ear from pulling on it so much."

"Well, as you can see, me and lil' man decided we'd stop by to see Unc' and this wonderful Neverland of yours before we made it out to the park."

"Maybe when I'm older, Unc', you'll let me and my girlfriend pop some popcorn and drink sodas while watching a movie."

Nard questioned, "You got a girlfriend, lil' man?"

"She's my school girl that I kiss whenever she ain't tryin' to beat up on me."

"And what daddy tell you to do when a girl tries to hit on you, son?"

"Pull out my wee-wee, show her and tell her that I'm the boy and she's the girl and that her place is taking care of me, not hitting on me."

"See what I mean," said Mike. "A pure genius."

"Whatever happened with you using that line with Mrs. Shenequa, sir?"

"Bra', it used to work perfectly back when we was younger until her height started exceeding mine by a few inches. She even grew some lengthy arms too! Kind of hard to get under them at times. What about you and ol' girl? She doing her own thang now?"

"Talkin' bout Peaches?"

"The one and only."

"Somewhat. We still bump heads from time to time."

"Make sure her ex-head ain't the one tryin' to bump yours with them lil' hot ones."

"The boy is doing huge thangs out there in them evil streets."

"But you wouldn't listen to yo' partna', though."

"I tried, homeboy. Lord knows I tried. But that night she was lookin' too damn good for me to let pass and the lord knows that also."

"So now we probably got divorces, courts and who knows what else, all because lil' head couldn't stay away from and out of the pants of Peaches."

"Never again and that's fa' sho'!"

"It's too late for that. What's done is done. Just make sure that back of yours is covered at all times. Especially whenever you're with her."

"That's mandatory but for some strange reason when we do be chillin' together, Shontae has a tendency of poppin' out my mouth."

"The one who's playin' hard to get," he said, sounding bewildered. "Let me find out them feelings of yours are starting to spill out."

"I don't know what it is but the shit is startin' to take its toll on a playa'. Excuse my French, lil' man."

"You aiight, Unc'! I'm hip to that and I know not to say it too."

"That's very smart of you, young man."

"One thang about the game," enlightened Mike. "If you ever decided to give it up physically and mentally, you'll always have what it takes to spit at whoever, whenever you feel like it."

"That's a part of me I'm going to the grave with. Though I do feel my body is takin' a turn for an early retirement. A brotha' thinks he's about to dig deep into Shontae's mind if I can ever get her to holla' at me."

"She actin' like that?"

"She thinking me and ol' girl got something going on. All I do is get at her from time to time, just to make sure she's still breathing. Something small."

"Sound like you might've laid the laws down pretty well with Peaches."

"You know a brotha' gotta do his best for the first impression. 'Specially with somethin' as bangin' as shawty. Now the rest is just whatever else we want to happen, happen."

"Look here. I think it's about time me and lil' man go out and sightsee some of the mothers and daughters for a while. Tell Unc' bye."

"Bye, Uncle Nard," he said, rushing for the front door.

"You running out our house without showin' Unc' some love? Come give me a hug."

Lil' man ran back and squeezed Nard around the neck before raising off the couch.

"Thank you very much, young man. Now go and keep it pimpy, pimpy."

"Aiight," he cheerfully replied.

"Is the palace still off the sightseeing list to yo' numerous shawty friends, including Peaches?"

"Most definitely. The rules ain't change just because I'm feelin' a lil' strange. Maybe with one and I mean only one, am I willing to bend a lil' for."

"It's all on you, playboy. Along with the crib."

"I should be through the way later on."

"I'll be there. As usual." He took a seat in his car. "Hold it down, Nard."

"Peace out, lil' man," yelled Nard from his door.

"Peace out, Unc'."

Lil' man threw up two fingers and rode down the street.

Chapter: 23

"We can't keep actin' like this."

"You right. Why I put up with your shit, I don't know."

"Yeah, you do. The time and love I invested in you is self-explanatory."

"But still I continue to play the roll of a fool and hang around. When are you going to take me more seriously and realize that I do have feelings like any other human being? You're hurting me. A lot."

"Why you cryin'?"

"Why you think I'm cryin'?"

"Cause your stomach hurts?"

She refused to continue to hear his gibberish and walked off.

"Wait! Wait a second! Don't do this to me!" He gave chase and snatched hold of her arm. She spun around. "If I wasn't serious about you, why would I have poured my all into you? Can you answer that?" He waited for a response. "I didn't think so. Well, since you so speechless for words, how 'bout answering this with one." He lowered to the ground on one knee. "Shontae Peterson...will you—"

He sprung out of his sleep. The waterbed made a loud splashing sound from within. Sweat poured down his forehead, leaving a trace of dampness on his pillow. Low, thumping sounds from his heart were loud inside the silent room. The stereo clock read 4:11 p.m. His head hung downward in a drooping posture. A sigh of relief gave him satisfaction, knowing it was just a dream.

He continued lying on his bed long after the dream, wondering what was wrong with him. How someone he hadn't seen in years stirred up memories that were supposedly long forgotten. Or he assumed. While at work, he thought about her. With his friends…in his sleep. Once, during sexual intercourse, she lingered in the back of his mind, forcing him to lose interest in his mate. The haunting effect bothered him deeply. No longer would he allow her to continue imprisoning his thoughts, or avoid him. He wanted to jump up, get dressed and search under every rock possible, if only he knew where to begin. Or remain civilized and try using her number for the second time this week. His eyes glued to the ceiling fan, contemplating on what he should do. From the fan to the phone, his head rotated. He snatched hold of the phone, dialed her number, and heard a ring. An answering machine clicked on. He patiently waited for her recorded voice to end before saying, "This is Nard. If you have any care in the world about me, meet me at Cooper Creek Park. 7 p.m. sharp! Peace."

He drove up to the park entrance sign, which read: Warning! This park forbids any of the following violations. Loud music, drugs/alcohol, violence, littering, a speed limit exceeding 5 miles. Anyone found in violation of the listed acts will be prosecuted and fined.

Over a thousand times, he'd entered the park without ever analyzing the words written on the large board. Today, everything about the area attracted his undivided attention. The booming sound escaping out of his trunk went on mute, and he finished off the remaining beer in his cup. Double matches of tennis in a fenced-in location to his right were the first sign of activity he observed. A kid on a bicycle crept up to his passenger window, shouting, "Hey, mister. Wanna race?" Nard patted the gas pedal, jerking his car forward. In a flash, the kid was off and paddling fast as he could without looking back. To his left were several couples jogging the 5 mile gravel track that stretched around the entire park. The reflection of the sunrays off the lake began to soften into a reddish blend, nearing its evening setting. Under a large patch of shades, overhanging the water banks, he parked.

Patiently, he waited. Five minutes early. Better ahead than behind was his motto. The clock continued to tick. His leg rested through the window frame. Waiting. Two beeping sounds alerted him of 7 o'clock, and yet…no sign of Shontae. Time moved slower. And slower. Silence was settling in around him. Thoughts racing. 7:05.

Off in a far distance in seclusion, she spied through the thickness of large hedges. She made it to the park shortly after him, deciding to play a game with his emotions first. His unsettled demeanor proved it was working. Both identified the time, which read twenty-five minutes after. No longer could he sit and wait, feeling like the fool of a lost cause. The brake lights to his car lit up, positioning his foot back inside. Successful in her plan, she watched him pull out onto the pavement, deciding to cross his path in traffic. Unsure of the woman driving in the opposite direction, he stopped and witnessed the car do the same. He reversed back to the driver's window.

"Is that sweat I see dripping down your forehead due to a workout, or have you been sitting in the sun impatiently waiting for me?"

"Woman, be fo' real. What gives you the impression that I've been trippin' 'bout yo' delay that's so damn late?"

"Probably the hostility in your voice."

"Me, mad! Not at all. Just angry as hell. But you did show up, and that's what counts."

"To hear your bullshit for the last time, probably, before I decide to call it quits altogether."

"Would you mind, then, if I try and make my first true impression felt tonight? Somewhat a social gathering. At my place. Say, around nine. Just us two. Give us both a lil' time to freshen up. I think I'm capable of keeping you fully intrigued on what it takes to make you say yes, not once, not twice, but forever and a day to me being a major factor in your life and dreams. Now, with you playing these kid games, I ask that you put it to the side and make this adventure one of your realist yet."

"And who are you to throw those 'kid games' up in my face when all you do is make game boards at your residence, all day and night?"

"Only to help me stay on point, baby girl. The world don't grow slower. Just check the internet. Check yo' phone too for my address. Anyway, hasta la vista."

Before she was allowed a response, he drove off. Her eyes dazzled in astonishment at how he left her in limbo, even after she played the trick on him first.

CHAPTER: 24

Vertical blended colors designed in his Coogie sweater presented class at its highest degree. Slacks worn of the same brand name were a background burgundy and baggy fitted. Prada dress shoes imported from overseas made out of the finest leather handcrafted by Indonesians. Small dabs of Channel Platinum Cologne rubbed in on his sweater. He noticed a half hour of free time left on his diamond trimmed Rolex. At that moment, horrifying to pleasing thoughts competed on the idea of her beauty in his comfort, wondering how the night might end. His laws of dating usually consisted of simplicity. Not tonight. Too much was at stake. It was mandatory he presented an impressive A-game or possibly lose out on her forever.

He re-examined his apparel in the mirror. His reflection broadcasted a bright future in modeling if he chose to venture off in its profession. He eased out of the bedroom to finish preparing the designated areas. Lit candles on a table fragranced the dining room with a coconut aroma. Pleased with the setting, he maneuvered towards a place of soft seating in his living room. The feeling grew unbearable for him to just stand and continue admiring what was rightfully his at a distance. Most homes he visited in the past forbade guests from sitting on furniture used for show and tell only. His personal views were the opposite of such lewd ideas and dove on his couch without a care in the world. "It's mine, god damn it, and I can basically do what I want to on it!" Unfortunately, his fun was intervened by a doorbell ring, signifying the beginning of a long night.

Readjusting his clothes, he approached the front door. The anxiety in his hand reached out for the handle. He snatched it back. Long, deep breaths slightly settled his nerves. Outside the peephole stood beauty displaying pure elegance. He partially cracked the door ajar, prolonging her entrance.

"Judging by the time on my watch, I would say," he lifted his wrist, "we are a lil' bit early."

"The last I heard, the early girl beats the wormy nerd. Not gets."

"Now, I've been called some hideous names before, but to be called a nerd...well, that takes the cake, young lady."

"If the glasses fit." She accompanied his smile.

"How about makin' a quick entrance inside before you use up all your jokes a lil' too fast too soon."

She stepped in, feeling him take ahold of her hand. The front portion of his home she partially viewed struck her mind with glee. He sat her down on the couch underneath a portrait of Harriet Tubman. Her mind was somewhat boggled on how someone she once considered a nuisance would turn out to be a man of such high quality. That was then. Tonight, she admired what he revealed to her so far.

"Nard?"

"Yes, beautiful."

"You don't mind me asking you this...but what cartel are you connected to?"

"Ooookay. If you must know. They're located in the yellow pages, and they go by two words: Mercedes Benz! Whatever you need, we will succeed."

"Very funny, sir."

"About as funny as that foolish question you just asked me. Unlike some Americans, I work for a living as a car salesman and I'm damn good, to be exact. Shontae, my time can be spent way better than killing off my own race, including myself. Personally, I don't know if I should take that offensive or not."

"I apologize, Nard, but your home is...and I hate to give you the big head about it...very nice."

"Thank you, and the home decorator thanks you also. Are there any more questions you would like to ask before I proceed with our plans for tonight?"

"No, sir. You may carry on."

"Now, you wanna know what's really nice? You allowing me the opportunity to feel like the luckiest man in the world."

"Puh-lease! If that's the best line you got to offer, this date will easily be a piece of cake."

"A piece of cake! What you thought that was some type of game I just spit?"

"You ain't know."

"It ain't even that type of party tonight. To say that took a lot of guts. Especially coming from me."

"So now I'm supposed to be touched by that comment?"

"You damn right! I'm serious when I say I do 'preciate you giving me this chance for us to know each other a lil' bit better."

"Don't go getting all sentimental on me this early in the evening."

"A brotha' is only trying to be himself without much of the bullshit. If you don't mind."

"I would really appreciate that, Nard."

"Ok then. Now that we got that established, can I offer you something to eat?"

"Well of course, sir."

"I have three different types of frozen dinners that you can choose from." His ears rang with her laughter, and he slid away. "Since I didn't know what you like and being that we're not going out to eat, the least I could do was give you a choice of the frozen ones and plus everybody eats them."

"Could you please bring out the menu?" She finished her laugh.

"Follow me, madam." A marble stovetop stationed in the center floor of his kitchen was decorated with yellow and red roses inside several vases. Dishes neatly stacked in racks by the sink under a window overlooking the spacious backyard. Pull-out cabinets in walnut were an added feature where he grabbed the drinking glasses out of. The platinum-stain refrigerator doors were wide enough for one to walk in opening its freezer side. "The lady's choice," he said, pointing at the selection. "Lasagna with broccoli and cheese, chicken and rice with gravy, or fish and macaroni?"

"A sista thinks she'll have the fish and macaroni."

"Dinner will be served in five minutes. Would you mind taking your seat at the dinner table through that door to your left?"

"Don't mind if I do."

More and more, her doubts about him started to fade. Stronger, her emotions grew. She continued to portray nonchalance.

She wondered if the setting would appear extravagant in its own appeal. Surveying the room's entirety as she entered left her speechless. Flames dance atop of lit candles on an octagon-shaped table, enlivening her senses. A mahogany China cabinet possessed ancient silverware with its large structure shadowing over half the dim room. The jazz tunes seeping from out of secrecy seized her attention. Her limbs began moving in a rhythmic-like motion to the soothing sounds. Beyond life troubles she managed to evade before hearing his voice shatter a perfect moment.

"Excuse me, Shontae."

Slowly, she responded, "Yes."

"Yo' choice of drinks are distilled water, Gatorade, Nouveau or Cristal."

"A Nouveau would be nice."

"Coming right up."

He returned, pushing a meal cart and drinks on ice underneath. Sliding out her chair, he requested she take a seat. Her food placed down in front and prepared her drink. To the opposite side he hurried, setting up his area.

"Dinner…is now served."

"Did you have any help coming up with this idea, or was it all your creation?"

He pointed to himself. "Yours in the flesh."

"How about a standing ovation for the mister."

"Please, please, have a seat. Save all the handclapping for the end. Right now, your food is getting cold."

They delved into their meals, continuing to share small talk. The majority of what was prepared had been devoured. She pushed her tray aside, satisfied at her consumption.

"That was very delicious, Nard."

"Is there anything else I can get you?"

"No, sir. But allow me to at least help you clean up."

"No can do. You're the guest, not the host. What you can do is escort your lovely self back into the living room and have a seat til' otherwise if that's cool with you."

"Your wish is my command, sir."

As she vanished out of view, he danced joyously, knowing it was a success. He was convinced the feelings were mutual, but knew through prior experience how tough she could be. He blew out the candles. The leftovers were dumped into a trash bag, which he carried out the back door. He regained his composure before taking a seat next to her on the couch.

"So what do you think?"

"Wonderful, Nard. Just wonderful."

"You know all of this is new to a brotha', right? I went beyond the extreme to prove to you how serious things can get. Only if you allow it."

"Nard, you are a beautiful person, and so far very creative too. But you have a tendency of roaming the jungle for too many females to mate with."

"A brotha' does have needs, as well as you do. Maybe not as much as mine, but you do have them."

"You right. I do."

"Being that, what I do is more of a sport-type thing with me leaving any feelings at home, the ones I been with in the past meant nothing to me. Also, I'm very protective when it comes to intercourse. Would you like to see my sexual disease status? One hundred percent clean of anything known to mankind."

"That's alright. I take your word."

"You should also take my word seriously when I say I'm ready to settle down with a woman that comes no closer than you, Miss Shontae Peterson."

Her face shifted away from him. She was undecided on a response. At the arch of her chin, his fingertip guided her head back around.

"Where is all of this coming from, Nard? Peaches done scared you from playing the games you supposedly play so well?"

"Peaches?! Shontae, you haven't heard a word I said, have you? I want you and only you. Nobody else."

"And how am I supposed to know that I'm not just another name being crossed off your list? Is there any way you can reassure me of that?"

"No. I can't."

"I didn't think so."

"But if you allow me to enter your world as I have allowed you to enter mine, well...you'll just have to trust me."

"Can I also trust you, the next time you see that female friend of yours, to tell her that if she ever disrupts me and my cousin's meal at the mall again like she did earlier today, I'm takin' off on her, starting at the face first."

"There was a conflict between the two of y'all recently?"

"She was very fortunate. My cousin just so happened to snatch my hand back right before I had a chance to scar up that pretty face of hers."

"Trust me, I had nothing to do with it."

"Yes, you did. Your name was the first thing she brought up. What are you sayin' to her about me, Nard?"

"Nothin', really. Except for how I always had a crush on you when we were kids. How it instantly reignited when I laid eyes on you again, how amazing and disturbing the feeling is knowing that you somehow managed to grow on me uncontrollably. And at this point, right here, right now, how my heart is ready to be placed in your hand, if you are willing to extend it out to me and rest it on your palm for eternal safety."

She tried discerning his words, distancing herself from him.

"What do you really want from me, Nard?"

He grabbed ahold of her hand.

"For the two of us to begin a beautiful friendship. I know you might need some time to analyze the scenario more clearly and whatnot, but all I ask is that as time progresses, our friendship escalates into something more than just friends. I'm feeling you, Shontae. I always have. As a matter of fact, I'm feeling you so much right now that I can't even feel my damn self." Her grip tightened on his hand. He flooded her space. "Excuse me for being so rude, but I need you. But only for the right reasons."

"If the feeling was mutual, would I still be able to sit next to you without you trying anything?"

"It's possible. Though I somewhat doubt if those guards you have up against me would allow it."

"If I let them down, you probably would try to take advantage of me."

"With the protection you have up around your domain, not even the armed forces could tear those walls down."

"You had to be handled in such a way cause this what I tote in between is pure and precious, allowing no dog in heat to just bounce up and down on me as if it's worthless."

"You have," he eyed between her thighs, "all of my approval on that one."

She nudged his shoulder, commenting, "What am I going to do with you, silly?"

"Allow me to begin a new introduction off like this." He planted his lips on hers. His tongue slid down her mouth, weakening her towards a merciless submission. He firmly grasped her face. In her mind, she yearned for more. She felt his mouth slowly begin to part from hers and pulled his face closer. He had her right where she belonged. Smothered in his strength. Embraced by her comfort. On cue, their mouths separated. "By beginning a new introduction with a kiss."

"Is that all you'll be beginning it off with?"

He swooped her into his arms and into the air.

"What are you doing? Where are you takin' me?"

"To a place that's built for preserving pure and precious jewels, baby."

Her fears had settled down once she had gotten into his cradling hold. The comforting fit resembled moments cherished in her father's arms as a child before he lost his life in a fatal car wreck. It devastated her to the point where she'd lived a good part of her youth in seclusion. Her mother had pleaded for her to come out of her room and go enjoy the sunshine. She seldom did. To school and home she traveled, day in and day out. Angel had managed to drag her along on ventures outside when she visited, which had become a regular occurrence. The great concerns towards her daughter's reclusive behavior had vanished thanks to her niece, and she enjoyed every minute of it.

Nard rested her feet on his bedroom floor. Their clothes were removed, piece by piece. Her nudity was pressed against his. She drifted in his strength once more, but was placed across his bed. The thought of caution froze his horny actions. An advantage to explore her temple had easily presented itself. A fling might've satisfied his sexual craving, but his heart longed for an eternal connection. Soul companionship. Exceeding any limits of his wildest imagination.

"Shontae, as we lay here, naked, preparing to make love, I ask of you, is this what you want? Are you truly comfortable with this? If not, I can remove myself if that's what will make you happy."

"Are you able to handle this? That's the question you need to be asking yourself."

"A lil' play-play before foreplay, I see."

"No! Another reassurance before disappointment."

"Well, may I begin such an adventurous journey around your world as we speak?"

"You need an escort with that trip?"

"Never that. Never that!"

Alright, Nard, he thought to himself. She's all yours. What's next? So much to hold. So much to choose from. How 'bout the shoulders first? Nah. Not enough flesh. Her breasts are firm and perky. Yeah! I'll lick her nipples for a while, then relocate elsewhere. Hello, tits! Excited to see me? Allow my introduction to be brief, but fulfilling. What's that? You said, 'What's the holdup?' Oh, here I come! And I mean right now.

She lay patiently, awaiting his first move.

"Is something wrong?"

"No, ma'am. Everything looks so…perfect."

He encircled as much of her breast as his mouth could hold. Down the center of her chest, he licked to the hair below her navel and paused. He glanced up at a set of white eyes through the darkness.

"She is one of the cleanest on planet Earth, sir Nard, and she also doesn't bite. Drip, maybe, but not bite."

Damn! This girl got more tricks than treats. No matter. In order to have what I need, a man must do what a man must do in order to succeed.

"Hand me those goggles on the side of the bed if you don't mind, Shontae."

"Ha, ha, ha! Wouldn't that be nice. Except for this trip you are headed on has a warning sign against anything that's not a part of the human body. Now, any last requests?"

His faced inched forward, inhaling the fragrance of her pubic area. He clutched her thighs underneath and looped his arms over top. She squirmed at the first touch of his tongue pressed softly to her clit. Her legs trembled in his clutch. The smothering force against his ears signaled the intense pleasure that she was enjoying. Panting sounds cried out. He inserted a finger into her vagina for added stimulation. The snug fit came as a surprise. "A virgin?" he pondered. "Impossible." A flowing release of ecstasy trickled out of her body and onto his chin.

"Is that how you like it, miss?"

She pulled at his head to where hers rested and frantically kissed away her juices off of his mouth. His midsection was partially moistened by her vaginal area, which caused an immediate erection. He figured a swift thrust within her without warning wouldn't cause much harm.

"NA—" she screamed out.

"So you are a virgin." Tears welled in her eyes. "How come you didn't say anything?"

"For you to laugh at me? Fat chance. It's a long story, Nard."

"And a long night. We got time."

"No, we don't. I'm starting to dry out, and I really would like to make love to you, but only if you be—"

He placed a finger to her lips. "Gentle. Yes baby. I promise."

He positioned only half of his lengthy erection into her, knowing the discomfort it would cause. The repeated practices of delicate strokes continued way past the minor pain she first experienced that eventually converted to an enjoyable feeling in her.

"WHOAH!"

"Just checkin'." She squeezed his buttocks in hopes of easing her mental unrest, which continued to linger. "All senses alert, I see."

Their sexual performance reconvened. The velocity of his thrusting slightly increased. Deeper penetration. Her hips in unison to his. Louder, her moans sounded, signaling an eruption of secretion. He climaxed shortly after her explosive release and rested across her shivering chest.

"Damn, girl," he said, nibbling on her ear. "I see why you kept me at a distance. Yo' loving is dangerous."

"You enjoyed yourself," she said, massaging his back.

"Did I!" He removed from off top to a position station beside her. "A brotha' is so drained right now that I believe if I tried to stand up and walk, it'll be like walking with two broke legs. Impossible!"

"You said you was ready for Shontae, so, she felt it was only necessary that she take you the distance."

"I believe you might've taken me too far." She crawled on top of him. "Ummm, Shontae. What are you doing?"

"Don't tell me you're finished?"

"No, ma'am!"

She sought life where he laid limp, and made a circular motion with her hips. His gradual swelling pressed to her vagina, somehow wriggling itself inside.

"Glad to see someone is still willing and able."

"From here on out, you and my man are on y'all own."

CHAPTER: 25

Shontae crawled out of his sleeping arms at dawn. The light sound of his snoring went undisturbed. She kissed him on the forehead, whispering, "Bye, baby," in his ear. A prayer accompanied her during the majority of the ride home for violating a promise made to her father, abstaining from sex until she wed. She struggled with a set of keys at her apartment door, sliding one in. The handle covered in mist disallowed her hand a sturdy grip. She wiped it dry with her shirt. It opened. Her eyes were troubled by the bright light shining outward. The weariness she experienced in her legs earlier had reoccurred. Inside against the door, she rested, awaiting for her strength to restore itself. Angel reclined out on the couch, preoccupied with her schoolwork. She acknowledged Shontae's presence and nodded, never once glancing in her direction. The continuance of her stillness eventually gained Angel's attention. She soon peeled herself off the door. Angel sat her paperwork on the ground, along with her feet.

"Well, good morning to you too, sista' gal."

"I'm sorry, Angel. Good morning."

She lingered in one spot near Angel, just staring.

"Have a seat, young lady. It won't bite." Angel waited for her to be seated. She questioned, "From the looks of things, it appears to me that someone held you hostage overnight, deciding to finally let you go."

Her blood was beginning to circulate back to its normal flow throughout her body. Angel detected life reemerging in Shontae's face. She sat peacefully next to her, acquainting herself with the thought of kidnapping a man's clothing.

"You mean, more like I had him hostage, begging for an early release."

She slid a pair of Nard's Versace boxers out of her purse.

"That's my girl! I knew you had it in you!"

CHAPTER: 26

Clear skies overlapping the city produced temperatures cooler than normal—upper seventies, with a light gust of wind. Nard spent the entire morning and late into the afternoon placing a glossier shine on his convertible. Tunes to the legendary Isley Brothers echoed out of his ride while in traffic. Mike rode in silence. He received a call earlier, having been informed to be ready once transportation arrived outside his home. A move Nard considered frivolous but worth a try. As usual, his delay worsened their chances in possibly avoiding a long wait in line at Carver Park Sunday gathering. He swung open the front door, viewing Mike in verbal conflict. Shenequa barked at his unannounced entrance. He waved, grabbed ahold of his friend, and fled the scene.

The trail of stylish cars in front and back of him wasn't as bad as Nard had predicted. Nor were they off schedule but only by fifteen to twenty minutes. The park wouldn't exceed its capacity until day shifted to night with about an hour of sunlight remaining. More than enough time for them to socialize or mingle amongst a chosen mate.

Lowering the music, he said, "Man, we fortunate. Ain't that many cars in front of us. It usually be hectic tryin' to make it in." Nard continued staring straight ahead without a response. "Aaah, damn. Here we go again. You with the silent treatment and me with the concern. Earth, callin' Nard. Come in."

"You—you say something?"

"Homeboy, you ain't said over a few words from the time you picked me up."

"You right."

His minor interest in conversing remained unchanged.

"Check this out. We ain't gotta go parlay up here at the park if you ain't into it."

Swiftly responding, "Bra', we about to post up in the middle of this bitch and do the usual…lay down laws."

"Well, act like it, young negro."

"Yo' man's just getting his thoughts together from last night. Shit was crucial for a playa'. I mean, while loungin' with shawty Shontae, she tried to break a playa' with the chocha. It's like, the golden rules that I live by didn't even exist with her. And here's anotha' wonderful story you won't believe. I still can't believe it. Shawty had a tragic experience in her life as a youngsta'. She lost her father at the age of nine. Shit wasn't the same with her after she told me. She stayed in her room. Wouldn't come out. It weakened her bad, she said. Her momma wasn't of any help or at least she avoided her mother. To school and home was all she knew. That is, until her cousin named Angel started to come around a year or so later, which slightly changed her ways to hangin' outside. To make a long story short, she promised her father she'd never give her love to a man until she wed, which would explain her ways in the past at school. And I always thought she felt like she was the shit. Look how wrong I was and a lot more of us."

"But she gave it up to you first. What made you so special?"

"Well, she said not only was I always funny to her in my own special way but very determined in life, similar to her father before he passed away."

"And that qualified you as the luckiest fella'. Sounds like you got a winner. Just try not to mess it up, man. Can you do that for me?"

"The way I acted last night seemed evident. She's the only one who knows of my location. Had me cook for her. Made love to her. Laid my head between her legs."

"Please tell me you didn't?"

"Did I! Hard to believe, ain't it. I know, I know."

"That's the shawty you been wantin' and look how lovely everything turned out for you. Damn! Did you see that!" He faced the outer direction as a flock of sexy women walked past his side. "Oh yeah, it's going down. Just look up ahead. This place is crunk."

They lingered in traffic at the park entrance. Crowds in conversation were seen spread over a wide range.

"Most definite. This is the best place to be right now for a lil' live entertainment." Out the rearview mirror, he noticed her five-foot nine slender waist sloping outward at her thick hips, just seconds away from bypassing him. He extended his arm outward. "Now, I know we ain't doin' it like that. Actin' like a brotha' don't exist in yo' world."

"Sir, do I know you?"

"You do now. They call me Nard. And you?"

"Olivia."

"O-live-it-up, you say. No problem. Hop on in." He cracked open his door.

"Not today, stranger."

"In due time, now that we know each other. But where's the temporary destination?"

"Nowhere in particular. Just walkin' around to see who can see me. That's all."

"Nah. That's not all. Judging by what my eyes can see, if I hadn't bumped into you, you was probably headed to a no-win situation kind of brotha'."

She checked the scenery before facing him.

"So who are you? The grand champion?"

"You ain't know! Me and my horsepower out-win them all from Mighty Mouse to Peter Paul. Enough with the small talk, being that a brotha' ain't tryin' to hold you up, but how can we make our next social gathering somewhat an anti-crowd event some way somehow?"

"Sure. Jot this down."

He reached between the seats into a small compartment.

"I'm listenin'."

"It's 331-2591. That's my Blackberry. My home number is 568-1801. And, sir," she said, placing her face in front of his, "whenever your motor is ready for the race, please be sure you pull up from behind next to mine."

The mini shorts she wore allowed a portion of her lower butt cheeks to expose themselves, bouncing loosely as she departed. Men heads extended out of car windows in hopes of a closer view as she passed.

"Shawty trippin', ain't she?" mentioned Mike.

"Pretty goddamn much. But as I was sayin', shawty last night, maaaan, I lost it all."

"Lost some or all?"

"All! ALL! From my composure. To the tongue. All the way down to the silk boxers I had just purchased for the occasion."

"Not the boxers too, playboy. Sounds like she might be tryin' to put a stump in yo' jump."

"I know."

He found a location where most of the spectators gathered and parked.

"But back to the matter at hand. I'm sayin', is it permanent or short-term, cause from what I've heard, coochie eatin' signifies a real playa' throwin' his towel in." Mike exited out of his seat and sped to the trunk for a refill of their cups. "My bad, Nard," he said, accidentally slamming the passenger door. "Lightweight material, you know."

"Keep that shit up and I'll see to it that you and your family reside somewhere on the corner of 21st and 2nd Avenue without a roof. Now, as I was sayin', a playa' just gotta wait and see. With all of the work I put in, she might place me all the way in my feelings if thangs turn out fo' the worst."

Mike's cup tilted toward his mouth, having paused it in mid-air. Her throwback swagger dressed in overall two-time her size and a backpack thrown across the shoulder added an unusual appeal, which complemented her beauty. The fitted cap she wore flattened her hair down the side to where it curved at the tips and bounced freely. He found her style a little outdated, but original. Her light brown complexion persuaded him enough to acquaint himself with her presence. The door flew open in front of her passing stride.

"Damn, slim!"

"Whooooah horsey! Must we be so violent! You gotta holla' at the owner of this ride for having push buttons that open these doors up so fast."

"Cut with the jokes, slim."

"So now you namin' a brotha'. Let me find out we cousins on Big Bertha's side of the family."

"Slim is just slang I use for the unknown, slim."

"You wouldn't mind, then, if I came up with slang for you, I suppose?"

"It depends."

"I kinda figured that. So this is what we can do. If I come up with a name that is pleasing to you, you hang around and we continue to enjoy each other's presence. If not, you walk off."

"Bet dat!"

She smiled at his ridiculous proposition.

He contemplated on a name before blurting, "Badass!" She wasted no time in making a departure. Mike rose to catch ahold of her. "I was just bullshittin'. No harm intended. Seriously, though. What's your name?"

"Anesha."

"That's a nice name. Different, but nice."

"My father named me that during my birth over in South Africa."

Nard remained seated in observance of Mike. His sight diverted off towards a huge commotion, encircling several cars on display, competing for the cleanest ride. Peaches waited, unseen, for an opportunity to surprise him. He searched inward and felt a set of arms embrace his neck. Her lips greeted his cheek at the moment he turned to recognize her.

"Hey, Nard!"

"This is how we doin' it now? In the public's eye?"

"Ain't no ring on this finger," she said, broadcasting her independency.

She moved to the side. He exit the car.

"It's only been, what? A month or so. Oh dude I know is still on the hunt for you." His body positioned against the door. She placed herself against him and whispered in his ear. He clutched ahold of her waist. "Is that how we feelin' right now?"

"You can't feel the stiffness in my nipples?"

The erection felt through his pants made her pressed harder up against him.

"I'm with you on that, but at this moment, let's chill. Aiight?"

"I can do that," she said, peeling herself loose.

Mike overheard them in conversation and glimpsed over at Nard's company.

"What's up, Peaches?"

"Mike, ain't it?"

"Something like that."

"Enjoying your friend's company. If he ever loosens up."

"Good luck."

"Now," she said, focusing completely on Nard, "where was I?"

"Bein' more careful on the things you do."

"IS THIS THE YOUNG CHUMP YOU BEEN DEALIN' WITH BEHIND MY BACK?"

His voice frightened her. Nard moved her to the side. They stood face to face. She stepped inbtween and attempted at shoving D-Man back. He wouldn't budge.

"You got me twisted, homeboy," stated Nard.

The tension intensified. They stood a couple of feet apart. Mike acknowledged his friend's trouble and quickly assisted him.

"What the hell's up, Nard?"

"Mind yo' damn business, boy," said D-Man.

D-Man watched the both take a fighting stand and took precaution.

Peaches walked up to him again, yelling, "What's wrong with you, D-Man?"

"I'm tryin' to see what the hell my lady thinks she's doin'."

"Will you quit sayin' that shit? I am not your lady. Leave me the hell alone." She pounded her fists across his chest.

"No problem. You got that."

He shoved her out of the way and vanished into the crowd.

"You aiight, Peaches?" asked Nard, comforting her in his arms.

"Somewhat," she said, wiping her face dry.

"Yo' ex is crazier than what I thought he was. Talkin' that slick shit out the mouth."

"Y'all straight," said Mike.

"We cool. Good lookin'. Peaches, this is the type of nonsense that I was tryin' to explain to you earlier 'bout yo' boy tryin' to make an unexpected approach."

"I'm gonna go and have a restraining order put on him."

"If it ain't handcuffs, not too much else is gonna hold him back from tryin' to impress, holla', or whatever he just called himself doin'."

"YO', PLAYBOY!"

The loud two words shouted over the crowd noise caught Nard's attention. Unable to pinpoint its direction, he continued to talk. He scanned the area again where he thought the voice might've come from and caught a glimpse of a husky male figure, possibly shielding someone. "POP...POP...POP!" The pointed barrel aimed at his torso, placed the first shot in his side. Nard's vision faded, fallen to the dirt. A stampede of spectators scattered. Dust flooded the air, making it impossible to see. Screams were heard in the distance.

"Pretty soon it'll be time for me to drive back to school, cause the semester ain't over with. Not by a long shot."

"Next time, I guess it will be the other way around with me picnicking at your apartment."

"So long as you and this Mr. Nard bring his twin. I'll definitely supply the meat," she said, expressing her humor. "By the way, have you heard from him today?"

"Not hardly, girl. After what I took him through last night, he might still be putting his feathers back together."

"I mean, did he ever get a chance to impress you?"

"The boy was jabbin' like Roy Jones in a ring. Quickly and deeply." She swung her fist in the air. "Angel, turn the TV up for a second, would you?"

"Why? What's up, girl?"

She pointed at the screen in serious concern. Angel pressed the volume on the remote. A man on a stretcher being loaded into an ambulance flashed along the screen.

The news caster was saying, "At about an hour ago, around the time of 7:15 p.m., a young man by the name of Bernard Hick was shot today while hanging out at Carver Park. Police have supposedly apprehended a suspect by the name of Jerome Darryl Jones. He was caught shortly after the incident once police was tipped off about the car he fled in. Jerome Jones, also known as D-Man, is believed to be the leader of an illegal drug ring known as the "Entourage". Bail has been posted at $1,000,000. As for the victim, he is reportedly in critical condition with a bullet wound to the right side of his lower abdomen. More details will follow on the 11 o'clock news tonight."

"You know any of those people?" Shontae sat motionless, staring at the screen. "You heard me? Snap out of it, girl!"

"The...the one who got...shot." Her face was contorted in shock. "That's Nard!"

"What are we waiting for, then?! Let's go see how he's doing."

Angel jumped to her feet. She slid on some shoes and raced to the door. Shontae remained glued to the couch, unable to move. Angel went back, pulling her cousin by the arm.

CHAPTER: 27

The room's pale design reflected its stale scent. Artificial flowers extending waist-high in a basket added no enhancement station next to the entrance. A two-seater couch threaded in wool fabric, occupied by Peaches, started to wear in certain areas. Nard laid on a narrow cot, asleep. Neatly tucked in white sheets, which stretched from his neck on down. It wasn't the best of comfort, but it did help him relax after a staggering process of surgery. Mike's worrying hadn't settled none. He paced back and forth in hopes of hearing his friend's voice. The incident continued to replay itself in his mind, having warned Nard in the past. "Don't even think about it, playboy. She's married!" And here he was, standing over his injured friend.

Neither Mike nor Peaches could fathom the horrific sight they'd witnessed. After the first shot had fired, Nard was blown to the ground. Peaches had yelled out in horror. Two more shots fired off into the dirt just inches away from his paralyzed frame. Mike positioned himself down low to rescue Nard. Both shielded him from the frantic crowd and waited on the ambulance Peaches had summoned.

"Muh—"

Mike gripped the bedrail and studied Nard's mouth. Peaches opened her eyes upon hearing his mumble.

"Come on, Nard! Say something, dawg. Anything."

She bowed, praying for his full recovery. Mike hadn't budged.

"Muh...Mary...Jane..."

"Not right now, homeboy," Mike said, smiling. "Maybe later." He rested a hand on Nard's arm. "This what I can't understand. If she don't love you anymore, be thorough! Why go through all that drama for a broad when he had the chance, took advantage of the chance, then abused it? Last I heard, three strikes and you're out."

"Some cats," Nard said, inhaling deeply, "get too ahead of themselves." He motioned at a cup of water that Mike had handed him and moistened his throat. "Thinking she might be theirs forever."

"I see," he said, lifting the sheet in observance of the patch on his side. "But check this out, the shawty I was kickin' it with at the park before 'the duke' went to gunnin' and runnin' at 'cha wanna creep and crawl after nightfall and I was wondering that since you and ol' Benzo ain't in need of each other tonight that—" He dangled Nard's car keys.

"You wanna ride her in my shit."

"Any questions?"

"Be—"

"You see? That's why we boys! We always see eye-to-eye on thangs." He rushed for the exit and spun around. "And, by the way, glad to see you aiight, homeboy."

Ms. Hick swung open the door a split second before Mike grabbed ahold of the handle. Nard's grandmother accompanied her.

"Hello ladies," greeted Mike.

"Tell me what happen, boy," demanded Ms. Hick, bypassing Mike.

"Short and simple, momma." He sat up with a slight struggle, but received help from his mother. "I was chillin' at the park with the young lady behind you when some cat, I mean a man, came up on us and started shootin'."

She glanced at Peaches.

"At least my baby is doing okay," said his grandmother. "That's what counts."

"Uh, uh, mother. I smell a rat. A fat one at that. Let me find out this foolishness was behind some fast-tale gal." Glancing at Peaches, she said, "No offense, young lady."

"None taken. But I did have some part in this catastrophe." She advanced towards Nard. "It was my recently divorced husband who shot your son. He saw us hanging together at the park and one thing led to another."

"One day, boy, you'll take heed to what I be tellin' that blockhead of yours," responded Ms. Hick.

She pinched his earlobe.

"Leave the poor child alone," said grandma. "Can't you see he's in enough pain already?

She released his ear.

"Thank you, grandma." He sneered at his mother. "Anyway, I should be leaving in a few days or so. So the doc says. The bullet traveled in and out, thank God."

"You get all the rest you need, son, cause me and your mother are just glad to see you are still alive." She placed a kiss on his forehead. "We don't want you leaving until you are one hundred percent."

Shontae entered the room, unannounced.

"Shontae!" His sudden upright position in bed increased his pain, forcing him back onto the pillow. "Shontae, how you know I was in here?"

"You was on television." She spotted Peaches out of the corner of her eye. "And what is she doing here, Nard?"

"It's a long story. By the way, momma, grandma, this is Shontae. Shontae, this is Ms. Jarrett, my grandmother, to the left of you, and to your right is Ms. Hick, better known as mom dukes."

"Hello, young lady," said grandma.

"Well, boy, me and grandma are gonna take it on home cause judging by the scene right now, the two of us might be out of place. Ain't that right, momma?"

"We sho' is, child. Take care of yourself, son, and when you get out of this mess you in with these ladies, give ol' grandma a holla'."

"Sure thing, grandma."

He knew of their past differences and hoped not to find himself interjecting in a brawl under his condition. At least not while his cot was the only thing keeping them separated. Shontae's discontent remained unchanged. Peaches ignored her for the most part, displaying minor signs of discomfort.

"Nard, will you please tell me why in the hell she is in here?"

"To make sure he's alright. And you?"

"No, Shontae!" He tugged at her lower arm, preventing her from approaching Peaches. "Calm down and I'll tell you, aiight," he said, holding her hand. "I was chillin' at the park and—"

"And I saw him sitting in his car and decided to talk to him. Minutes later, my ex-husband walked up, being disrespectful towards him, and I told him to leave. Not long after, he came back with a gun and started shooting."

"So if he hadn't been around you, none of this shit would've happened. Nard, why do you continue to deal with this woman?"

"She's a friend, Shontae. Just like you're a friend."

"The hell you mean, a friend! I ain't got to hang around and hear this lame mess you talkin' 'bout. Come on, Angel!"

"Shontae! Wait! Why you actin' like this?"

"Why am I actin' like this?" She walked back to his bedside. Her frustration shifted to a moment of doubts. Regrets. Fears! Rather she had actually been misused, or was some sort of specimen in one of his experiments. She shook loose the dreadful thoughts and tried concealing her sorrow. "'You would be too if you were madly in love with someone you thought might've felt the same damn way about you."

She sped through the door, shielding the pain that formed along her slender cheekbones.

"Hi, Nard! My name is Angel. Shontae's cousin. Glad to meet you. Heard so much about you. Hope you get well soon. Stay strong, black man. Goodbye."

"Damn," he said, pounding his fist into the mat. "What was you thinking when you said that?"

Peaches grabbed ahold of his hand. He snatched it free.

"Not right now, aiight."

"I'm sorry I've caused all this drama in your life, Nard."

"Not as half as sorry as I am for being so damn careless."

"Is there anything I can do for you?"

"No offense, but," lowering his eyes, "leave."

She wanted to be a friend in his time of need, but yet…it seemed as though that wasn't enough. She respected his wish without delay. She lifted herself off the couch and walked to the foot of his bed. A final glimpse of him gave her an unforgettable memory. "Bye, Nard," she whispered.

The handcuffs nailed to his swollen wrist added intense pain to the discomfort of being crammed in the backseat of a patrol car. His past involvement with the law some eighteen years ago landed him twelve months inside a juvenile detention center for fracturing a drug addict's skull. The sentencing judge labeled it a "heinous act of unexplainable cruelty to humankind" but spared him under the condition of having no immediate family throughout most of his life. He rode in remembrance of those cold, reek infested nights the gated location held him hostage within, identical to his next destination. He found himself fretting at the thought of losing his freedom. The one phone call permitted him before his admission would free him before a constable requested him to spread his butt cheeks and asked him to cough.

As planned, he shuffled through several papers, branding his John Hancock at the bottom of each. The sheriff responsible for handling D-Man's paperwork watched on in disgust at what he knew to be a dangerous man being released back into society. He was deeply perplexed at how the judicial system could tolerate such corporate injustice dictated by money.

D-Man downed a third of brandy he kept stored in the glove compartment, hoping to cleanse his thoughts of prison, past and present. Its content consumed at a rate exceeding three times the normal limit. Heavy rain bounced off the windshield. Lightning bolts parted the dark skies. For an hour, he drove around, undecided on how to inform his superiors of the careless mistake that was made, possibly jeopardizing the flow of currency, or halting the business altogether, which the family wouldn't tolerate under any conditions.

He fumbled the phone around in his drunken hands, punching in some numbers. It clapped him upside the head and rested on his ear.

"Mess…up…messed up…" He was drooling. "I messed… muh-messed…up."

"We already know. A costly one at that. Over what? A woman! D-Man, D-Man, D-Man. What are we going to do with you, my boy?"

Killing him seemed to be the best option. B.B. didn't need D-Man's troubles spilling over into the cartel. "We can't afford to lose you. Not now. Too much at stake. I'll make a phone call to one of my confidants in the district attorney's office. He'll probably play a major role in the case. Direct him to a couple of important people located elsewhere, and we'll go from there."

"Them say I…JUG DEALER! ME! And-and…a leader!" He swerved out of the way, avoiding a slow-moving vehicle that was pulling out in traffic. "All left to do izz leave TOWN! Fed's washing me. The-they…washin' me." He slammed on the breaks and skidded forward under the red light. "Come mornin'…I'm gone! B…somewhere… some…where." He saw a hand waving to his left, peering closer and bumping his head on the window. "Call…you back. Stay close by yo' phone." He slid down his window. Staring inside a black 1964 Impala covered in tint made it almost impossible to identify the man's face inching outward. "Where my…money…nigga!"

"Calm down, D. I got that right here. You want it?"

"Uh, you DAMN RIGHT! I want…ALL!"

"Aiight, aiight. Here you go. Catch!" Both hands slid outside the car window, gripped tight to his closest companions. "POP! POP! POP! POP! PO! PA-PA-POP!"

Bullets riddled through his body from head to toe. He had no chance to dodge the rapid fire, nor had he even been aware of what was held in the man's hands. No matter. Life after death only held such an answer for D-Man. The crime area remained numb, except for the sound of water trickling down drains. At a steady pace, the Impala crept forward. D-Man rolled off into a fire hydrant. His body slumped across the steering wheel. The life of Jerome Darryl Jones was no more.

CHAPTER: 28

Early Friday morning. The sun was less than half an hour from awakening the city. Nard tossed and turned for most of the night. His body was sore after a week-long rest on top of hard springs. His bags were packed, awaited an eight o'clock departure. His bandages had been replaced yesterday, but were marked with a red spot. Had it not been for the change in shirts, he wouldn't have noticed. A doctor examining him re-stitched the two-inch wound. They ran several tests on the inflicted area, making sure the damage wasn't internal. His rough sleep had ripped loose a portion of skin, which delayed his freedom for one more night.

The sight of the busy downtown district reminded him of just how thankful he was to be alive. The sound of horns honking attracted his attention without aggravation. Passing traffickers seemed friendlier. Pedestrians' loud voices flooding the sidewalks seemed more harmonic. Even the harsh odor of the polluted outdoor air served its own purpose. His entire outlook on life had changed, and he felt blessed to continue being a part of it.

Nard's first stop involved getting his scraggly beard reshaped to its normal sharpness at the barbershop and later on would pay his hairstylist a visit. The shop lacked its weekend crowdedness. A woman in her late twenties and two sons waited on Slim. Big Hick was almost finished with his customer. T-Funk was nowhere to be found.

"Have a seat, lil' bra'," smiled Big Hick, wiping hair out of his chair. "That life of yours came very close to receiving them daisies on a yearly basis."

Slim stated, "And you wonder why they say the 'womb' kills over a thousand ways in the playing fields."

"Who would've figured," replied Nard.

"Apparently, somebody who felt you didn't know any better," mentioned Big Hick.

"Good morning, gentlemen," entered 7-O.

"Mr. 7-0, we got a young man that likes to jump the fences of the most sacred wedding vows," Big Hick said, pointing at Nard.

"Is that so?"

"A bullet here. A scar there. You know," intervened Slim, "the usual."

"Damn, son! I see you haven't been schooled very well."

"Good thang he's still around so you can give him some of that ol' fashioned Parker Brothers game with the easy 1-2-3 instructions," joked Slim.

"The basics are the best foundation."

"You might be right," responded Big Hick.

"Ain't no such thing as might. It's either fo' sho', or no sho'. The brotha' tried to wound you in the leg? The hip? What?"

Nard brushed the hair off of his collar and tipped Big Hick. He lifted his shirt up, allowing everyone to view the patch. Smaller bandages protruded underneath a large one, covering a fair portion of his side.

"Kill shot," blurted Slim and Big Hick.

"From the looks of things, son, you out there playing games instead of playing 'the' game."

"Fo' real," he said, releasing his shirt.

"You mind if the two of us step outside and talk for a minute?"

"I'm cool with that."

"Excuse us, gentlemen."

"7-0, make sure my lil' bra' returns with game control instead of straw hats and ol' clothes."

The heat outside had increased some. Perspiration settled in fast under Nard's armpits. They noticed a pecan tree overhanging the side of the building and lingered under it.

"Son, we all make mistakes when starting off young, trying to prove to ourselves 'I'm the man' or 'this shit is easy'."

A woman dressed in skimpy attire escorting a child inside distracted Nard's attention. 7-0 quickly smacked the back of his head.

"Damn, pops! Are you crazy, ol' man?"

"Pay attention, boy! You see how easy it is to be caught off-guard when you ain't focused, but on bullshit." The anger in Nard's eyes soon subsided. 7-0 hadn't been fazed by it one bit. "When I first started off as a youngsta', I was just like you, tryin' to be the front man, letting nothing pass me by...from single women to married ones. Whatever had a poonanny, I was in it." He lifted a pant leg above his knee. "See this here? One in the lower shin and the other one on the side of my calf. Dam near blew all of the tissue out of it." His lower leg was half the size of his right one. "Just like you. Wanting to prove a point to myself, as if I'm the man. I learned quick that being the man only gets you stripped of the man faster than when you started."

"The relationship we had was nothin' serious. Just a small thing. Me and shawty havin' a lil' fun while living life on the run."

"Did the fun consist of you, her, and her man, all laid out together?"

"Hell nah, pops!"

"Well then, it's only having fun when everyone agrees on it at the table. But until then, this," he tugged at the skin on his arm, "this, is ALL TOO REAL! Young man, have you ever wondered why the owners of professional sport teams mainly overlook the whole playing field from high-rise booths? I'll tell you why. Because nine times out of ten, they started off calling shots behind closed doors, which elevated them to the top away from all the drama and news reporters and tvs and anything that would over-exploit them or their businesses. Don't always try to be in the center of it all because sometimes your eyes will focus only on what stands in front of you and not what goes on around you and that's definitely no good, young blood."

"I feel you on that, ol' school."

"Keep it up with the nonsense, and that's not all you gonna continue to feel." He extended out his open palm. Nard squeezed it with a firm handshake. "You seem to be one that's all ears and willing to learn so I'll make this short and sweet. Don't try running to them all. Definitely leave all the married ones alone. Last but not least, which is the sweetest of them all…the prize in the eyes can be your worst surprise if you are more infatuated on the outside instead of what's in the inside. Understanding brings wisdom, and with wisdom comes a lifetime full of blessings. Can you dig it?"

"All the way."

"Good. Cause any mo' of this good shit and the meter clicks on at a hundred dollars a minute. Well, I'm going back inside for a while, where I shall continue to humor myself at the foolishness the young generation be talkin' out the side of their mouth."

"Appreciate yo' hospitality, 7-0."

"It's only right, young blood, that I share my experience with you. That's just the playa's way. From the old and gifted to the young ones with good intentions."

"Is everything aiight, 7-0?" asked Big Hick, noticing them walk back in.

"Only time will tell, young man."

"Yo' fellas, I'm headed out. Good lookin' on the cut, Big Hick. Y'all hold it down."

"Believe that," assured Slim.

"Keep hope alive, lil' bra, or is it, try and stay alive."

"Both. Be easy, 7-0."

"You do the same and remember, young blood…the game chose you. Don't lose it!"

"Beep! Beep! Beep!"

Nard's radio drowned out the blaring horn. Her headlights flicked on and off, signaling for him to stop. For more than a quarter mile, she'd trailed him down Fort Benning Road on south side Columbus. He glimpsed in the mirror, noticing her closeness, but continued driving. Making out the individual through shades and a ball cap made the task that much more difficult. She sped up within inches of his bumper again. He decided to pull over at an upcoming gas station. The angered woman exited her car faster than Nard could place his in park.

"Who in the hell do you think I am? Some type of whore?"

She swung at his head. He managed to evade a few of her blows, but he felt one graze his earlobe. Leaping out of his convertible, he scooped her up and placed her over his shoulder. The beating continued across his back.

"Felicia! What is wrong with you, woman?"

"Put me down! Put me down, you…womanizer!"

He placed her in the front seat of her car. His hand held both her slender wrists tightly together. The strengthening clasp made her cry out in pain. With his other free hand, he slid her legs inside and shut the door.

"Shawty, are you crazy?"

"I can't believe I let you get me in my feelings like this and for what? All because I was stupid?" She broke down in tears. "Are you happy now? I mean, at least you could've called to see how I been doing or something. Anything to let me know you haven't forgotten about me or I wasn't just some type of fling you was out experimenting with."

"I'm sayin', what's it been, like, three or four weeks?"

"Four weeks from today and thirteen hours, to be exact."

Nard laughed. "Damn."

"Will you quit with the bullshit?" snapped Felicia.

"What you want from a nigga, huh? You want me to whip my shit out and give it to you right here, right now? What? Is that what you want?"

"All I wanted was a simple hello, Nard." She noticed the serious pain he was experiencing express itself over his face. "What's wrong, Nard? You okay?"

"Yeah, yeah, I'm fine," he said, massaging his side. "I'm sayin', though, you wanna see my face all scratched up?" He brushed her hair with his hand. "That wouldn't be nice, now, would it?" She shook her head. "I didn't think so. So why swing on me all because we let our feelings get in the way?"

"Because I hate you," she said, playfully slapping his hand.

"I hate that you hate me for hatin' yo'self."

"You got all the sense, don't you?"

"Not really. And yes, I do apologize, Felicia. A brotha' never meant to take advantage of you. But, unfortunately, I let the big head outthink the bigger head, stepping on your feelings, as we can see."

"Why me?"

"Why not you? I figured, at the time, you was easy prey."

"You know you owe me, right?"

"You right. I do. How can this foolish man make up for such a foolish act he caused?"

"First, you could start by buying me a soda and some chips."

"And then?" Her lips rested against his ear, whispering what she demanded out of him. "I'll be right back!"

He sprinted inside and was out in less than a minute, handing her the items she requested. In his laid-back seating position, he tailgated her down memory lane.

CHAPTER: 29

"Hawk Eyes calling Home-Front, over."

"Go 'head, Hawk Eyes."

"Suspect now hanging out in front of Sandpipers Apartment on East Street, over."

"Roger that, Hawk Eyes."

"He appears to be loading up a vehicle with suitcases that are more than likely filled with clothes. The description of the vehicle is a maroon four-door Taurus. A newer version with an Alabama plate that reads…" He raised his binoculars.

"MJG-187," informed Agent Buck.

"MJG-187, over." Agent Thompson released the button to the receiver. "Thank you, buddy."

"Hey, wat are crackers…I mean…partners for?"

"Will need assistance in the area as soon as possible. Over."

"10-4, Hawk Eyes."

"Over and out." He positioned the radio in its case. "Looks like the birdie is about to try and fly the coop on us, ol' pal. Except, this birdie flies without wings, making him an easy prey to catch."

"About as easy as him leaving a small trace of DNA on a couple of them shells. Come on John! Let's take this young punk down! Right here! Right now! Damn his shooting sprees!"

Agent Buck swiftly unsnapped his holster and twirled the 45 chrome-plated Magnum around his forefinger. A trick he mastered as a child while watching "Billy the Kid". The loud click-clack alerted

Agent Thompson that one had been loaded into the barrel of his coworker's gun.

"Calm down, my friend. We don't want to kill him in cold blood if we don't have to. At least not in front of those kids inside the car with him."

Thompson and Buck, two veterans of the GBI (Georgia Bureau of Investigators), staked out in an unmarked car one block down. Vehicles parked on the side of the road, shielding their hidden agendas. One desperately sought the moment to use brute force. Agent Thompson preferred the cat and mouse game, which overruled his partner's mayhem. 2-Piece's criminal file was displayed on their computer screen, which had revealed information from prior shootouts. One involved a policeman. They were certain the fugitive would further his spree if they presented even the slightest apprehension. Reinforcement seemed the wiser choice. Back at the station, Chief Roberts demanded the suspect behind bars, unharmed, until his dying days. Both knew the consequences for disobeying the chief's direct orders.

"Hand me that suitcase, J."

"Man, I still can't believe you out like this. You know the streets ain't gonna be the same without you."

J-Dub assisted him with the last piece of luggage. The overstuffed trunk eventually closed after several tries. 2-Piece's son stuck his head out through the window, glad they had finished.

"Will yo' mans ever see you again?"

"Maybe, J. But for right now, though, I gotta get ghost."

"You might wanna do it fast. Your son is starting to look at me all crazy."

J-Dub felt a great loss of friendship release from within his arms. He continued hanging around long enough to see 2-Piece strap his seatbelt on. The chances of ever seeing his friend again were slim. A reality that was hard for him to accept. The dreadful pain forced him to walk off.

"Ay, J!" He stared back at a set of keys thrown in the air, which he caught hold of. Some belonged to 2-Piece's cars, and one to his former apartment, prepaid in advance for the next two years. "The keys to the city we built, homeboy. Finish lockin' it down for us."

"By all means, partna'," displaying a broad smile, "by all means."

"Our suspect has now pulled off. I repeat, our suspect has now pulled off. We are in pursuit, trailing him until we get assistance, over."

"Roger that, Hawk Eyes. Assistance en route."

"Maybe this one has intentions on crossing the state line on us," assumed Buck.

"Not if I can help it. If I'm not mistaken, they're going to try to catch the exit a few blocks ahead."

"Which would probably be less of a hassle if we set a road block on the expressway."

"Now you're thinking."

"All we have to do now is make it to the highway up the street, baby, and we're home free."

"Daddy," spoke his son, sliding his head between the front seats. "Are you coming home for good?"

Facing his kids, "Would y'all like that?"

"YEAAAAAH," chanted his son and daughter.

"They really do miss you, Marcus. And so do I."

"I believe you, Tonya. From here on out, it's just the four of us." He rested a hand on the side of her neck and shoulder blade, massaging away any doubts she might've had of him leaving. "See that exit up ahead on yo' right? Turn off at it."

"Well, well, well," said Thompson, securing his receiver. "Hawk Eyes to Home Front, over."

"Go 'head, Hawk Eyes."

"Suspect has now turned off down the ramp of Exit 3. I repeat, Exit 3. Have me a road block set up between Exit 7 and 8, pronto. You copy that?"

"Copy that, Hawk Eyes."

Buck spotted extra help in unmarked cars, approaching from the rear.

"Let's let the games begin, shall we?" He secured a tight hold on his gun.

The speeding traffic slowed. Tonya's concern forced 2-Piece out of his reclined position as she tried to discern the scenario up ahead. His face moved inward, closer to the windshield. Patrolmen stationed on the left and right shoulders were checking for identification.

"Daddy, what's wrong?"

"Nothin', honey. Daddy will fix it."

Traffic came to a complete stop. Patrolmen were squatted, guns pointed. A trap! Nowhere to run, nowhere to hide. "How in the—" he whispered to himself. He'd spent the entire day wiping clean any fingerprints off the bullets loaded into each clip. Then the thought had hit him…hard. The last two shells were marked with his kisses before he inserted them into each chamber.

"We have you surrounded, Marcus Smith! Step out of the vehicle with your hands up!"

"Marcus! What's going on, honey? Please tell me something!"

"Kids, Daddy wants y'all to always remember," he said, viewing the fear in their eyes, "that he will always love y'all."

He reached around and embraced them with one arm.

"This is your final warning! Step out of the car with your hands up!"

2-Piece tuned out Tonya's frantic shouting and focused inward on his fierce thoughts. With every blink, he saw flashes of bloodshed… possibly his own. But not without a fight. Not without defending his life to the very end. He glimpsed into his kids' eyes one last time in an unspoken goodbye. His daughter was crying. His son's face displayed fury, prepared to defend his father at any cost. Police continued to wait, motionless. Options were irrelevant. Hell before jail was tattooed across his chest. He slid a hand on the door handle and surveyed the entire area. The sound it made as it unlatched crawled into his mind. A gust of wind whistled past his ear, making its way inside. The solid weight that once pressed to his seat left only a mark in the leather material.

"Freeze! Freeze! Get down! Get down! Now!"

The officers scrambled to their feet. 2-Piece leaped over the side rails, running up the grassy slope. Safety had presented itself too far off for him to hide among trees. Instead, he braced himself for warfare. In a split second, he ripped open the button-down plaid shirt, freeing loose his closest friends. Rapid gunfire pointed at the crowd, rupturing an officer's cranium and leaving him slumped across the rails. Another shot clipped one in the neck. Blood squirted on the vest of a coworker within arm's reach of the victim's falling body. Agent Buck knelt low for protection. A clear aim focused in on his target. The first shot fired fractured 2-Piece's wrist, forcing him to shake loose one of the guns. Another shot blasted through his kneecap. Stumbling, he stared menacingly through the eyes of each barrel as more shots riddled his body. The battle had ended. The war was over. He held his middle finger to the sky with a final "fuck y'all" to the officers. Not a moment too soon, the final shot tore through his mouth.

"DAAAAAAAAAAAAAAADDY!"

His kids watched in horror, hoping their slain father had survived. For most of the confrontation, Tonya had kept her face hidden. Now, a glimpse at his frame face down in the dirt drove her hysterical. Her head pounded against the steering wheel, nearly knocking her unconscious.

CHAPTER: 30

It was only fair he follow her to her residence and proceed in accomplishing a fulfilling task. They made it inside her condo. Thrilled by his aggression, she rendered herself helpless, pent against the door, the keys still dangling out of its slot. Her tongue twirled passionately around in his mouth. Feet lifted off the ground. Buttons unfastened. She slid down his boxers and pants far enough for them to finish falling on their own. His hand underneath her Dereon summer dress untied the knot in her thong. He spread her legs apart for more comfort in preparation of his entrance.

For several seconds, he paused to analyze the hunger on her face, the impatience dancing in her eyes. It informed him how badly she wanted it. Wanted him. He shifted his waist, his erection searching for her vagina. She felt his swelling surpass her sultry entrance and she released a moan of pleasure. Her hands lowered to his side, squeezing him tightly, unaware of his wound. The pain forced him to stiffen. He bit down, easing the intense pain. Agony dared to intervene in his thrusting, but he remained focused on his duties. An eruption of pleasure landed her shivering on his chest. Finishing his task, he rested her feet on the floor.

"Now," she said, nibbling on his neck, "was that so hard for you to do?"

"Not at all. But next time, just be careful at how you swing those hands of yours at a brotha'."

"Sorry 'bout that, baby," she said, wiping a streak of sweat off his forehead.

"I know it was just a spur of the moment type thang. Yo' feelings got touched, and hopefully this somewhat smoothed out the rough edges between us."

"Take care of yourself, Nard."

"You do the same."

"Now that you know where I reside, please feel free to stop by anytime," she said, kissing his lips.

"Will do, shawty."

"Now go…and get the hell out of my place before I turn into the Gensu knife killer, cutting your dick off first," she said, clutching ahold of his penis.

"I'm gone out the door," he said, shielding his midsection with his pants, "faster than one can say 'gooood damn!'"

CHAPTER: 31

Peaches' heavy sobbing lasted the first half of his funeral. Many nights she wished bad things would have happened to him, but never death. Not in a million years. A closed casket prevented her from viewing his face, where bullets had blown out his eyeballs. Only once was she allowed a glimpse of him at the morgue to identify the remaining corpse of Jerome Darryl Jones.

His corrupt lifestyle had finally caught up with him at the crossroads of a brutal ending. The act of rape she believed he attempted to perform on her was downright intolerable. She couldn't imagine in her wildest dreams why he had wanted to lash out at her in such a horrible way. "I hate yo' ass, D-Man!" was all she had practiced in her mind once the wedding ring had been removed from her finger. Such disgust and hate had made it that much easier to move on with her life. But somewhere, hidden inside her, was an ounce of love she kept secretly stored away for him. They had been married for almost a decade. He was her closest family, except for her mother, who was only a few miles away. Their ties weren't as strong as she would've liked them to be, but nonetheless, her mother was blood, and that was all that mattered. The other 90% of her family was born and raised in California. A place she visited as a child on a couple of occasions.

The preacher stood over his casket, reciting the ending prayers: "Let not our sins capture our spirits, but entrap our own ignorance, for God does not forsaketh all who acknowledges his welcoming arms! May you rest in peace... Dear brother!"

The forest, which sheltered its setting open up enough space to accept the coffin lowered in its hole. A marbled green casket allowed the sun to reflect its shininess entirely as the pallbearer ended his job. In gold, Greek letters written on top were the words: "Cross my heart, no time to die...D-Man's Game," identical to the words on his back.

Peaches wasn't a bit surprised at the handful of people who attended his burial. Two men of Columbian ethnicity, both short and of a stocky built, mumbled under their breath the whole time. One even paused to communicate on his phone for a brief moment while the preacher spoke. She placed them as D-Man's higher affiliates by the past description he had given her. Seeing the men walk in her direction, fear overtook her body. Was it money he might have owed, she wondered, and they were coming to confront her about it, or something worse? Her feet felt planted in the ground below her, unable to step forward or backward. The men stopped, shared their condolences, and kept walking. Her heart racing out of control, it finally slowed to its normal rate. She bowed in prayer for forgiveness of anyone her husband may have inflicted pain upon, including herself.

CHAPTER: 32

"For the last few weeks, yo' butt has been going out with Nard all the time, and not me. Would you mind explaining the reason why, sir?"

"For one, you always pick the wrong time for us to do our thang."

"But here you are, always expecting me to give your horny ass some sex. Mother always told me that a fool in need is a fool indeed."

"You my girl! I'm not expecting you to do anything. Definitely of nothing that comes natural of any couple. I'm sure yo' mother told you that also."

"Any couple who acts like a couple. Not like strangers. Move, boy! Get the hell off me!"

She disallowed him a chance at placing himself on top of her. He sat back on the couch next to her with a puzzled expression.

"Come on, baby! Ya' boy horny! Why you trippin'? It ain't like we don't go out sometimes and mingle like lovers supposed to. You know I ain't goin' nowhere. So why trip?"

"Why trip? Because my supposed-to-be-man acts as if our ties are only due to me being your son's mother." The longer she talked, the more her words faded into gibberish in his ears. "That's exactly what I'm sayin'! Give me that shit!"

She snatched the remote out of his hand and pressed the off switch.

"Woman, you done went and bumped yo' damn head. Cut that back on."

"That's exactly the type of nonsense I'm talkin' 'bout right there. This TV gets more out of you than me. Here, nigga!"

The thrown remote bounced off his thigh and landed on the floor by his foot.

"You break it and the next one comin' out yo' paycheck, sistah-gal."

"Mike," she said, standing over him. "I've had enough time to weigh the good, the bad, and the ugly between us lately, and the majority weighs more in favor of the ugly."

"How can you complain when we both work, bills are always paid on time, and on top of that, lil' man is straight. From my scales of justice, I would say I fared pretty damn good."

"Boy, if you don't wipe that smirk look off your face, my backhand is gon' slap you so hard, people gon' think Don Juan done changed the game from pimp slap to bitch smack."

He rose to his feet, leaving a thin margin of space between them. "Aiight, woman! Joke's over."

"Negro, who said I'm jokin'?" Her cold glare penetrated through his pupils. "When we first met, you was so…real! Now, you gottin' to be nothin' but a pain in the ass."

"You think so?"

"I know so. Mike, I'm this close," she spaced her index finger and thumb about a centimeter apart, "from leaving you."

"There's the door. What's stoppin' you?" A knock at the door interrupted their argument. "Yeah! Who that?"

"Nard!"

"Come in!"

Her case in point proved right. Where he wanted to be more was standing outside her home, preparing to enter. She dared remain in the same room with Nard and stormed to the back.

"Did she just run out of the room cause my breath stinks or what?"

"Nah, man. Not only is she actin' like her period is on, but she's also on one of those 'let's hang out' sicknesses again."

"How 'bout I holla' back at a better time when things are much better."

"Don't wait up for me, Mike." She stormed past them.

"Where do you think you're headed, woman? I ain't through with you yet!"

"Out!"

"Drive careful," yelled Nard. Her response came in the form of a middle finger. The slamming door knocked down a family portrait, shattering its glass. "I love you too!"

"You know you got a fool for a baby daddy, don't you? A short one at that. He really don't mean you no good, girl. I believe you gone crazy. Or he done put roots on you or something. Whatever it is, he got Shenequa wrapped around his pinky."

"A damn fool is what you sound like. Shenequa is nobody's fool. What I want is for our child to not have to experience the single-parent relationship. Is that so much to ask? My parents have lasted over thirty-eight years strong. Why can't I?"

"That's because in those days, women weren't wives. They were house slaves, entrapped by the chores and the responsibility of raising kids. Time has changed, girl. We, women, have better opportunities now. Independency is the thang, baby, and even if you are single, they got wonderful sex toys to help us calm our nerves without hearing the bs that comes out of a man's mouth. I don't know about you, but I'm very cool with the way the new millennium has turned out."

"I feel you, girl, but I have a lil' ol' school in me. I prefer to try and work things out. Our problems haven't been too burdensome. Thank God! At least, not yet. Shit, my parents had problems, true enough, but love conquered it all. Why can't ours?"

"You see! See what you just said! Love! Something he ain't got for you. Maybe unseen, but definitely not visual."

Shenequa rode alone for about an hour in search of peace of mind, deciding to pick up Meka. She cruised around town, contemplating where her life might've went wrong. She and Mike had withstood some of the toughest times imaginable. His love for her was never the factor, but hanging out in the streets were. The problem sometimes worried her senseless. Since falling in love as teenagers, she vowed to keep their ties strong through thick and thin. Reality partially outweighed her strength tonight. Doubts of continuance in the relationship settled in.

"Have you ever thought about what life for you and lil' man would be like without him?"

"Not really."

"I think now might be the perfect time. I mean, look at you. You look like a nervous wreck. It's obvious he can't seem to realize that the dumbness of his daily activity between the two of you is startin' to take its toll for the worse on my Nubian queen."

She placed her hands on Shenequa's shoulders, massaging her friend's frustrations.

"That feels good, girl."

"I bet he don't even take the time out anymore to try and help ease the tension you're feeling right now." She sat up on her knees, placed in the seat for a better position. The ongoing massaging relaxed Shenequa completely. They stopped at a red light, unaware of its sudden change to green. The warming touch of Meka's hand placed sight of her friend's lowered eyelids and lips in greeting of hers. "I'm sorry, Shenequa. It's…I don't know what I was thinking." The night skies hid her shame. For so long, she tried concealing her affection for the same sex from her friends. Her flesh weakened at Shenequa's hurt. Avoided she practiced but fell victim to the oily skin surrounding Shenequa's neck, awaking her hunger. "Please forgive me for being so stupid."

"Meka," said Shenequa, embracing her hand, "where would you like to finish this?"

"You know, Mike, I sit and try to analyze and better understand yo' predicament with Shenequa and I came up with one conclusion: Help! Cause that, my friend, you need plenty of."

"Thanks for the advice, friend! What I do need help with is a refill of this pitcher with with more Corona. Excuse me, Miss Beautiful?"

Her height was a possible inch or two taller than his, wearing three-inch heels. A bra for a top piece only shielding her breasts, which matched the thong she pranced around in. Slanted eyes enhanced her Latina appeal. Brownish and gold streaks of hair passed her shoulders, dancing with every stride taken. She had the figure of a goddess.

"Yes, how can I serve you?"

"Oh, serve me you can. Refill me, I need. Corona, please. Thank you, baby."

"If only every man could enjoy so much nakedness in one spot at a time, the world wouldn't have all these clone-type George Bushes running around tyrin' to corrupt and destroy every damn thing."

"You said a mouthful, then. As soon as she returns, I'll have to drink to that."

"Would any of you fellas like a lap dance?"

"Hmmm, do you mean us gentlemen?" Nard curiously questioned. "Not at this moment, but I tell you what. If you can come up with a better approach in sellin' yo'self, I'll give you fifty dollas' and you can keep the chain and the lap dance."

"Are you serious?"

"Child," said the waitress, overhearing Nard's last statement, "the only thing these girls got on they minds is bustin' they legs open as wide as they can."

The stripper balled up her fist in the waitress's face as she walked past.

"Forget her, shawty. She just hatin'. But you tryin' to get paid or what?"

"Sure."

Nard snatched a vacant seat at a table nearby and placed it at the front of theirs.

"Here. Have a seat for a minute. This won't take long." He admired the way her thighs spread out over the chair. "What's your name, cutie?"

"Cocktail."

"I'll drank to that, too," commented Mike, downing the beer in his cup.

Foxy Brown Nude Club offered many women resembling Cocktail. Her weight was of a solid but firm structure. Her height exceeded almost six feet. She was a light shade of walnut brown without a noticeable flaw. Her hair was jet black and silky. Her bra struggled to hold in her double D breasts from protruding out the sides.

Nard asked, "How long have you been doing this, and do you plan to make a career out of it?"

"About eight months and yes, I do."

"If you keep that weak introduction up in selling yo'self, you'll only bring in enough loose change to get you back and forth to work. Your whole approach was on some boredom as if you're programmed with no game plan about yo'self."

"What would you prefer? For me to just jump off in your lap like this," she placed her body across his lap, "wrap my arms around your neck like this then start grinding on you and later on ask, 'hi, big boy, you want a lap dance?'" His face was covered by her large breasts.

"That's a start," he said, hugging her waist. "The object of the game is to not only let yo' body do the talking, but to hypnotize the mind as well. Once that happens, the rest is sure to follow on through ensnaring their every thought." She slid back over in her chair. "Upon your introduction to a stranger, make sure what he wants first is a lap dance. Ask him if he's straight. Is he satisfied with the choice of women? You know, communicate first. Then you go for the profit." He rubbed his hand on her thigh. "The way you approached me tonight was a big turn off. Try to sound a lil' more convincing with your words. Show me you enjoy my presence along with what you're doing and that it's not just all about my money between the two of us."

"Damn that bullshit he talkin', shawty," interrupted Mike. "I got fifty-one dollas' for a lap dance right now if you cut him short."

"I ain't gonna hold you up any longer, Cocktail, but always remember this: What you say to a person will always have a bigger impact than what you show them."

"What did you say your name was?" She placed her chair under the table.

"I didn't. But for you, Daddy."

"Okay, Daddy. Thank you for the advice." She kissed his cheek.

"Anytime, sexy."

"How 'bout I give you a lap dance on the house?"

"Yeah!" demanded Mike. "Lemme get that."

Nard nodded for her to perform the act on his friend. Mike's legs extended out in front of him. She outweighed Shenequa by at least fifteen to twenty pounds, and his weakening lower limbs felt every bit of it.

"I'm straight, shawty. 'Preciate that."

"What can I say." He felt pleased with his influence on Cocktail.

"If only I could get Shenequa to listen to me like that. Things would be much better between us."

"In yo' predicament, that goes both ways with the two of y'all coming up with some type of understanding."

"You right 'bout that. Her agreeing to my every wish."

"First of all, you gotta quit takin' y'all relationship for a joke and know that what you're doing not only has an impact on her, but on your son as well."

"Now you wanna be the good fella up in here all of a sudden."

"Not really. I wanna see you do the right thing with her. That's all."

Mike straightened up in his seat and leaned inward.

"When you start caring 'bout what goes on between us?"

"When reality started drippin' out my side."

"So now you want my life to change all because you done felt some pain, due to your mistake?"

"How much longer can we continue to play the field? Til' we ol' and gray with a cane all off in the ol' folks' home, grabbin' Miss Daisy across the lower part of her back? Cause an ass, she ain't gone have."

"Hardly a lower back, either. To be honest with you and myself, a brotha' do got a lot of love for her. Cause if I didn't, I would've been choked her out a long time ago and that's that."

"So what you waitin' on?"

"What you mean, what I'm waitin' on?"

"You don't think it's 'bout time you got at her with the bling-bling?"

"Marriage?!" His laughter, accompanied with a hard pound on the unsteady table, attracted the majority of the club's attention. The pitcher spilled a small amount of its content. "Sorry 'bout that, everybody. Funny joke I just heard."

"All I'm tryin' to do is be straight up with you. What you decide from here on out is on you." He lifted his cup to his mouth, mentioning, "But don't say I didn't warn you, cause she's still someone that I find to be very attractive."

He knew the remark would stir up friction between them, and shielded his smile with the cup. Mike's finger rested in front of Nard's nose.

"Watch it, playboy. You try that slick shit if you wanna, and I'll personally bury that ass of yours myself fo' reassurance of yo' breathless life."

"Calm down, peeps. I got way more than enough on my plate to deal with than to try and step on my right-hand man's toes like that." They sat speechless for a while before deciding to amend the strife he'd initiated. "You gon' sit quiet on yo' boy for the rest of the night or what?"

"You know that was dead wrong of you, right?"

"From playa' to playa', I'm sorry if you felt like I violated you." Mike just stared at Nard's hand lingering in the air, finally deciding to clasp ahold of it. "My nigga'," smiled Nard. "I got love for you like my brothas', Mike. Always remember that."

"I think it might be time for me to straighten up my act a lil' and take our relationship a lot more serious."

"It's your call, homeboy. But don't forget about lil' man. Now hold me down a quick second while I go relieve myself." His journey shortened, returning back to the table. "Mike, I knew I forgot to tell you something earlier when I first got to yo' crib."

"What's up, playboy?"

"The fool who tried to end my life at the park last week, somebody put the finishing touches to his the same night he tried doing away with mines at a red light in his car."

"Damn! They doin' it like that in C-Town now! On some Crenshaw gangsta' shit!"

"And who said bullets ain't got no one's name on 'em?" He stepped off.

167

CHAPTER: 33

2:03 a.m. Her imagination was running rampant. The fragrance of a woman's nakedness pressed to hers sent chills down her spine. She indulged in such an act out of curiosity, not desire. Meka's flesh clutched softly to hers, an enjoyable moment. One she dared not adventure ever again in her lifetime, which was more than what she could say for her friend. How Meka's preference for women over men evaded her and possibly Tosha's long-term friendship remained a mystery. Forty-five minutes ago, a true side of her exposed invited Shenequa along for the ride. A woman's touch brought fun. Her man, deeper pleasure. Deciding Mike over Meka lacked any substance. What was at home shared bad times, but unexpectedly created good ones.

The sight of her darkened home was a relief. Her shoes were removed at the front door, as she didn't want to make a sound on her way inside. She entered the hallway bathroom. A rag rinsed under scorching hot water removed the stain of her friend's lips off of her face. In her mind, she envisioned taking a shower, but opposed the thought of the splashing sounds running water would make. She decided it was safer at dawn to finish rinsing away the remaining traces of a night well forgotten.

Light tapping sounds of footsteps alerted her ears. The steps grew heavier as they neared outside the door. Too heavy to be her son. Her hands gripped tighter to the sink, frightened by his entrance. "Damn it, Mike! You scared the shit out of me!" Their eyes made contact in the mirror. She wasn't sure if he caught a glimpse of a cheater or his son's mother. He shifted her around. Her body positioned against the counter.

"I been in the room, listenin' to music, just chillin'. Waitin' for you to come home. Good thang I got up makin' sure the house was straight cause I was just about to doze off."

"Mike. I—"

"Hear me out, baby. Let me go first and you later. Earlier today, I acted like a fool knowing all that I think, sleep, and dream about is you." He wrapped her in his arms. "We been doing this going on about twelve years and in the past few hours I've had enough time to think about what I'm about to do." He knelt down on one knee, embracing her left hand. "Shenequa Jackson...will you marry me?" Her mouth widened, startled, unable to express a sound. "Don't answer it right now. Think about that while I give you something else to think about."

Mike peeled loose her clothes off around her waist. He still marveled at how her stomach lacked any stretch marks after giving birth to their seven pound, six ounce healthy boy. His mind refocused on the sight of her pubic area. Her leg lifted on his shoulder, spreading the aroma of sex he knew nothing about.

"Mike! Baby! Please...don't "

But she succumbed to the enjoyment of his tongue wiping clean her vagina.

CHAPTER: 34

If only he could've been more cautious with the careless choice of words spoken to Shontae, he wouldn't have been hanging out in the parking lot of her apartment, hoping for a chance at correcting his wrong. To grant her the pleasure in leaving his life without a fight was not going to happen. The decision made today had to be accomplished. He figured maybe her seeing him in person would awaken something inside her and hopefully not hate. She'd refused to acknowledge his past calls. His brief messages flooded her answering machine to no avail. The only choice remaining was a knock on her door. A task he found challenging. One thing remained clear: he needed her, and it was all that mattered.

The first couple of knocks were feeble. He tried it a second time, but harder.

"Who is it?"

A chance at manning up to his wrong spoke loud and clear. He stared at the door, awaiting for her to open it. His sight converted towards the ground at her flawless feet. Her thighs partially covered by boy-shorts. The door slammed in his face before he could make eye contact with her.

"Shontae! Baby! Please! Don't do this to me!"

"Why are you here, Nard?"

"You know why I'm here! It's you I seek, my queen!"

"Save that corny ass line for someone interested, Nard."

"All I want is to tell you what's on my mind real quick, Shontae, and after that, I'll be out of your way."

"Make it quick, and you got sixty seconds starting." She held her watch up for the second hand to reach twelve. "Now!" He cleared his throat. "Fifty-five seconds and counting."

"Aiight, aiight! Here it goes. I want to first apologize for what happened at the hospital with that silly remark I made. That was very inconsiderate of me."

"You damn right! And?"

"And what we experienced at my place between the two of us, I felt, was a brief introduction of what could possibly escalate into something wonderful."

"A brief introduction?"

"Yeah. You know, boy meets girl. Boy shares feelings and girl feels guilty. Both experience body touches."

"Too bad this girl is grown and the boy is still childish."

"Oooh, that was cold."

"Twenty seconds and counting."

"To make this long story short, I have feelings for you. Deep ones. Mentally, I'm turned on by none other than you. Ever since that night, my whole world has been crippled, blinded, and got me actin' crazy as hell. You make me weak in ways that I can't even begin to explain. What I'm sayin' is...I got a lot of love for you girl. There! Are you satisfied now? Have a nice day."

He hadn't thought twice about hanging outside her door for a response and departed down the stairs. The door swung open. She raced to the rails outside her door, yelling, "Nard!" He looked back at her from the bottom of the steps. "Aaaaaah, that was soo sweet!" She ran to where he stood. He stumbled backwards, catching ahold of her as she leapt into his arms.

"Woman, you gone quit making this difficult for me."

"Would you prefer to work for something well deserved or received too easy?"

"Pertaining to you, I'd have to say both."

"If you say so, big baby."

CHAPTER: 35

Three hundred and fifty-nine days later into a new year and Mercedes Benz dealership clientele had continued to increase. Record-breaking sales, number one distributor within a four-hundred square-mile radius and nationwide recognition ranked it amongst the top five in America. A normal Monday for the average dealership hosted few, if any customers. Mercedes Benz mornings started with several purchases, ranging from sixty to ninety thousand dollars, and Nard partook in one of the sales. He wanted to break for lunch but possible buyers continued entering the lot. A white, elderly man dressed in worn-out overalls and a straw hat opened the door to a 2015 C Class that guided Nard in his direction. The customer's outer appearance might've displayed ashyness, but, in Nard's line of work, it was what lay on the inside of a person's pocket that was where their true description was secretly kept.

"Good afternoon, sir, and welcome to Mercedes Benz car lot, where the rides are your surprise and your cash is my life!"

The overweight man struggled to his feet. He accepted Nard's greeting in an offensive manner. His dry, pale face darkened to a reddish shade of fury. Nard quickly went to reciting the job manual in his head, which helped him remain calm and practice politeness with a customer, regardless of their hostility.

"Look here…boy!"

Nard checked to the left and right side, in search of a third party. "Excuse me, sir?"

His head slid back out of harm's way from the man's pointed finger directed at his nose.

"I brought yo' porch monkey asses over here to this country and I'll damn sure as hell take you back, boy. Even if I have to do it by myself. You hear me!"

Nard's mind snapped into a frenzy.

"What did you just say ol' man? Pops, bwoooy, I'm about one second from shoving my foot up yo' fat—"

"Hooooold on, Mr. Hick!" A salesman nearby overheard their verbal altercation and stepped between them. "I'll take it from here, Mr. Hick. Thank you. Now, how can I be of some assistance, sir?"

"You can start by getting this afro-a-negro away from me."

"You want some of me, pops? Huh? Come on! Take your best shot!" He pounded his fist on his chest.

His coworker shoved him back further. In his mind, Nard pictured himself beating the man into a coma, but he'd experienced worse scenarios at work, deciding to overlook the customer's ignorance. He readjusted his tie and caught a glimpse of a woman's perfectly shaped derriere faced upward, leaning her body across the driver's seat. She fumbled around on the passenger side, unaware of his presence behind her.

"Good afternoon, young lady. So please, tell me, how can a brotha' like me be of some assistance with helping a woman like you?"

"Hello, Nard." She slid herself outward. "Well, are you just gonna stand there in shock as if you just seen a ghost or can a lady get a hug?"

"Umm, yeah. I mean, damn, Peaches. What, it's been like, a year now?"

"Yep. Since the last time we was together at the hospital."

"You right. What happened to you?"

"I decided it was best that I give you what you wanted."

"But I didn't mean for this long, shawty."

"What can I say? My presence was bringing too much drama into your life. But, here I am."

"And still beautiful. So what's the latest and greatest with you and your life now?"

"You know. Taking care of my own. Working. Being independent. Raising a child. Basically the usual."

"Hold up. What was that last statement you just made?"

"The usual."

"Nah. Before that."

"What, raising a—"

"Bingo!"

"I have a son, Nard." She walked over to the passenger side and unbuckled the baby out of his carrier. He trailed her. "You see him? Ain't he adorable?"

"Cute lil' fella'. Mind if I hold him?"

"Sure." She extended out her arm.

"What's his name?"

"Kedar Bernard Johnson."

"Please tell me you kiddin', right?"

"A few days before we had sex, I had just come off my menstrual cycle. You was the only one afterward. Matter of fact it's really like I been celibate when I found out I was pregnant."

"The rubber! It was on! It couldn't have ripped. Or did it?"

"I guess it must've with you doing it so good and me tightening my vagina around your every stroke, that'll do it."

"He has everything but my last name." He led them up to his office. The baby rested snugly in his arm, rocking back and forth in a seat behind his desk. He sucked on a bottle with his eyes partially opened. "You know we gonna have to go and get a blood test?"

"Whenever you're ready, Nard. Any day is available for me."

"And here I am, about one week away from being married, and now this."

"Congratulations. Hopefully your wife will be understanding now that you have a son in your life. By the way, who's the lucky one?"

"Shontae."

"Mm."

"And what's that supposed to mean?"

"Nothin'."

"Yes, it does. I know that sound in your voice." He rose to his feet and walked in her direction. "Listen to me. I don't want no problems out of you. In other words, let me tell her about what's going on, and you stay as far away as possible from her until I let you know things are cool."

She stood to her feet, embracing them both in a tight hug.

"Don't we make a cute family?" She planted her lips against his. The move influenced a continuance on his part, but guilt drove him back. "What's wrong, baby? Mommy don't turn Daddy on anymore?"

"Yes! I mean, no!" He found himself pent next to the wall. She placed his arm around her lower back. The office door appeared too far off for him to run through, disallowing him a chance at a possible escape. "Peaches," he said, fumbling for a business card in his shirt pocket. "Here! Get back in touch with me so we can go take the test and we'll go from there."

"We missed you, Daddy."

"Card. Appointment. Next week."

"Kedar, say bye-bye to Daddy."

"Bye, Kedar," he said, handing her the baby.

He shut the door behind them and sat, confused, at his desk. A fine time for his life to be divided into halves. Shontae had mellowed down tremendously after his proposal several months ago. Her mind knew of only Nard and his smile ever since moving in with him. Maybe she would handle their problems like lovers were supposed to or maybe he stood a better chance at surviving by jumping out of a twenty story building without a parachute. Anyway, he contemplated on the situation. He lived smack dab in the middle of it all. His mother's words were replaying in his head. "Boy, you are a product of what you make. Eat it!" Today, it all started to taste like shit.

CHAPTER: 36

"Kedar Bernard Johnson!"

"Can you believe it? The whole scene of that night still replays itself in my mind, clearer than anything else. Including our wedding tomorrow."

"What are you gonna do?"

"What I'm gonna do is more like what can I do?"

"Head for the border while you still got a chance?" The seriousness in Nard's eyes made Mike feel uncomfortable. "Sorry 'bout that, bra'. But are you even sure the baby is yours?"

"We took a blood test. 99.9%."

"Lord, have no-no's on this man's soul."

"Judging by the time on my watch, I would say we got about eighteen hours and some change left before we end it the playa's way to doing it the family way."

"Welcome to the club, pops," he said, patting Nard across his back. "Even though I got you to blame for all the rings and things, yo' boy ain't trippin' at all."

"You played your part about as much as I played mine."

"Tell me who this sound like. 'What you waitin' on, man? Gone and do the right thing, man!'"

"It's either that or pulling up to some shawty's house in a wheelchair, demanding the rest of our money before she gets rolled over."

"One thang bout it, that girl of yours wasted no time in putting that big ball of chain around yo' ankles."

"How could I refuse! Shawty got more bags of tricks than Lucky got Charmes. Ain't no tellin' what to expect with her when the lights go off."

"Just don't let the whips and chains be a surprise when they do come back on."

"In that case, she must finto' do magic and use that shit on herself."

"You know, playa', it ain't gonna be the same, not payin' our usual respect to this great place of double D's anymore."

"While we're here, we might as well make the best of it."

"Starting off by admiring that sweet and chocolate with her Spanish-fly friend at the bar."

"See how easy they made it for us. Not only is she sitting at my favorite spot at the bar, but she just ordered my favorite drink."

"What are we waitin' on, then?"

"I'm waitin' for her glass to depart itself from her mouth and after a few seconds, ol Mr. Bay-Bay should have her mind spinning around and around in a daze."

"You mean like, out of control."

"Need I say more."

"After you, sir."

Mike directed a clearance for Nard to pass him first. The ladies were astounded by their surprise greeting. They ordered the gentlemen similar drinks and carried on small talk in a secretive huddle.

Shontae knew the elastic cloth tightly shielding her eyes wasn't the kind of fun she was used to participating in and sat motionless in Shenequa's passenger seat. It didn't take much for their mutual relationship to strengthen into closer friends. After nights of dining out together, becoming more acquainted with each other, one always found the other in need of company for a night out on the town. Nard became perplexed at how quickly she'd taken a liking to Shenequa. The lady-like mannerisms Shenequa went to displaying while indulged in their social gathering had Mike wondering where this part of her sprung form. "My mother taught me way before I met you, Mike, on how one must grow to be a lady of style and class and not act like a lady with only just a fat ass!" Shontae couldn't have agreed more with her friend's remark in the past, and figured no harm could be involved in playing along with Shenequa's game tonight.

The suspense Shontae was experiencing had her requesting a number of times what the event pertained to. Shenequa eventually replied, "Girlfriend, listen…what lies ahead of us tonight will never be displayed in this way again." The car parked on side of the curb at their destination. Shenequa raced to the other side, escorting her friend out.

"Watch yo' step, girl."

"How I let your silly tail trick me into this mess, I have the slightest idea."

"Easy. It's our last night of freedom and I decided the best way to end it is not only a bang, but with a ka'pow as well!"

Tosha dressed in a baby phat t-shirt and sweat pants slid across the floor in house shoes, responding to the knock at the front door. The giggling sounds Shontae heard knew they pertained to her being blinded. Pulled inside by the arms, Tosha led her into the basement. Women preoccupying chairs were lined up beside the wall. Furniture moved out of its original place to the far corner for a giant, white cake that read "Surprise brides" in big letters.

"Okay, ladies! Calm down! Calm down!" Tosha stood next to the cake, awaiting on every one to quiet down. "Aiight, ladies. With us tonight are two very soon-to-be brides. To make this speech real quick, cause I'm startin' to get impatient myself, Shenequa, would you do the honors in removing the cloth from around her face?" Shontae stared at the sight of the enormous cake. "Single and soon-to-be-married woman, without further ado, I present to you," she pressed on the button on the radio, "Candyman!"

At the sound of his name, a man burst out from the top of the cake, wearing a g-string and a bowtie. Shontae's heart pounded rapidly in her chest. His bulky physique and carved abs were more than she could handle, and fell back into a chair. He walked over to where she was, lifting her out the seat. The stripper began dancing throughout the entire room. The ladies made a circle and threw money at him. Shenequa and Tosha observed from a distance, laughing.

CHAPTER: 37

The pianist keyed a soft tune while in observance of guests flooding inside the tabernacle. Girls and boys of shortest to tallest heights in separate lines prepared their entrance through the double doors. Two toddlers leading in front tossed a mixture of white, pink and red rose pedals to the floor. Empty pews in the very front were filled up with kids parting in opposite directions. Girls to the left. Boys on the right.

Shenequa's arm held around her father's was escorted inside first. Her pearly white dress ballooned outwards at the midsection and on to the floor. The upper garment styled in a v-shape from across her shoulder on down exposed a minor portion of cleavage. Underneath her veil were teary eyes that she fought back from falling. Shontae, guided in on the arm of Big Hick, wore a gown identical but with a lighter shade of pink. Standing in patience, the brides awaited the grooms' presence.

Increasing whispers began to exceed above the low chatter. The brides surveyed the room in serious concern of the grooms' late arrivals. No one had seen nor knew of their whereabouts. To everyone's surprise, lil' man came bursting through the closed doors and ran to where the pianist sat, mumbling in his ear. The man nodded and repositioned himself. His fingers played to the sounds of "Superfly" escaping out of speakers installed through the walls. Shontae noticed the preacher failed attempt at hiding his smile. Shenequa pointed in direction of the entrance, where Mike and Nard were leaning in a stance against both doors. Tilted brims atop of their heads with a feather on the side. Jackets thrown on their shoulders, held by a finger. Slowly they walked.

Standing ovations erupted inside. They reached the podium and signaled for quietness. The grooms clapped once. Two women entered through the side door, taking hold of their hats and jackets. They clapped twice, receiving a kiss on their cheek, which the ladies then departed from afterwards. Another eruption of applause forced the grooms to turn and bow to the audience.

The wedding reception held on the bottom floor of Marriott Hotel furnished caterers in white tuxedos. Over three hundred family and friends attended in a vicinity spacious enough for an additional two hundred. Identical wedding cakes of three feet stationed on a lengthy table surrounded by food were covered in chocolate and white icing designs. A marshmallow sketch of the bride and groom's faces pressed together at the highest point. Shontae rested comfortably on Nard's lap at their table. He fed her small portions of cake when he wasn't too busy shaking hands. Shenequa's and Mike's mouths separated for a water break at random. Her finger dipped in some icing off her plate and smeared it across Mike's top lip. He held her face up to his, where the icing marked her nose.

"At the wedding, whose idea was that, Nard?" questioned Shontae.

"Me and my man played our parts fifty-fifty. We felt we had to take it back to our playa's root and respect game."

"Now that all player cards have been folded, can I have a juicy kiss my married man is supposed to give me?"

"Don't do it, homeboy," warned Nard. "Them two lil' boys standing by the food at the end of the table have been watching our women since the time we sat over here. One even licked his tongue out at me. Look at 'em." They noticed the devious smiles on their faces. One held up his fist. The other unrolled his middle finger. "To be so young and be that much of a playa' hata' is gon' be crucial on them when they bad asses get exposed in the years to come."

Shenequa stated, "They are kind of cute. Aren't they, Shontae?"

"You don't mind sharing, do you, Nard?"

"Not at all, beautiful. As long as you and Tiny Tim can fit together in a single-size casket, don't let me stop you."

"Congratulations, everybody!"

"Meka! What's up, girl?" Shenequa stumbled over Mike's foot, trying to reach her friend. "Long time no see. I'm glad you could make it."

"Shenequa, is it alright if I talk to you in private?"

"Sure. Mike, baby, will y'all please excuse me for a minute."

"Make sure you know how to find yo' way back into my arms, baby girl."

"For a minute there, I thought the girl might've fallen off the face of this earth," mentioned Nard.

"Who knows what happened to shawty. Last I heard, she was brushing up against bushes that leaked when trimmed right. Ouch!" Shontae smacked his shoulder. "What! I can't help it if she finds the former wrestler Chyna Doll more pleasing than the boy next door."

"If that's what she prefers, that's her business," said Shontae.

"Excuse me, stranger, but can I have this dance?"

Ms. Hick's joy switched to disgust, identifying his unwanted presence. Ms. Jarrett stood amongst their circle of relatives, encouraging her daughter to loosen up and go enjoy herself. She humbly refused his offer by saying, "HELL...NO!" Escorting her daughter out to the center floor, she signaled for him to come join them.

"Here you go, son," she said, extending Ms. Hick's arm out to him. "The two of y'all are way past due for a reacquaintance anyway. Have fun, kids."

"Mother, I'm gonna deal with you later."

"As I was sayin' earlier, miss, may I have this dance?"

"Just long as you keep yo' flirty ass hands above my waist and below my chest, I don't see why not. But only for one song."

"You always were the bossy type."

"And you the flirty one."

181

"Only because you cold-shouldered me six and a half days out of the week."

"Make that six and two-thirds out of a week."

"However you like it, young lady. But how have you been doing lately?"

"Lonely, but proud of it."

"You and me both."

"Not the founding father of 'I get around' part one. What happened to the young skeezy you ran off with to Disney World? Mickey take her from you?"

"Somewhat. But Minnie made up by giving me money for food and taxi fare to get back home and here I stand. Right where I was meant to be."

"Hold on a minute, slick. You screwed up the best thing you ever had in your life. Not me. Don't let this friendly dance go to yo' head."

"It's not the dance, but the," he sniffed her sensual fragrance, "perfume that's doing it. You smell very wonderful tonight, and look beautiful, too, in your dress."

He held her tighter. His comforting grasp reminded her just how long it had been since she was held in such a way. Thoughts of good times they once experienced danced through her mind. Life brought mistakes to some of the best-behaved people she knew, and wondered rather if his could actually be forgivable.

"This is wrong," she said, freeing herself loose. "You hurt me, Johnny, and here you stand in front of me, wanting to reignite ol' flames. Why you tryin' me like this? Why haven't you just moved on with your life? Why bother mines?"

"To be honest with you, I don't even know. Our son invited me and I gladly accepted it. And there you stood. Someone I truly used to enjoy and actually never stopped loving. Sometimes, a person's greed can cause him or her internal bleeding. Well, I've bled long enough and maybe you 'll never stop but I will say this." He held her back in his arms. "I do still love you, woman, regardless of how much you might hate me."

"I need a drink."

"You never drank anything before in your life. When did this start?"

"Right now."

She went over to where drinks were being served. Mr. Hick followed. The caterer extended her a glass, but he intercepted it, placing the alcohol down on the table.

"Barbara, you know damn well I am not about to let you do this to yourself, but lord knows if I'm the cause of it all...allow me to make an exit. Have a good night, Miss Hick."

"Wait a minute, Johnny. Just wait." She watched him turn to face her. "If, and lord knows if, the chance ever presented itself for us to get involved with each other again, we'd be friends only. Just friends! You understand me, Mr. Johnny? Friends, I said, and maybe, just maybe, if I wake up one morning and somehow accidentally bump my head that causes me to actually forget who in the hell I am, then there's a small possibility that your unthoughtful past ignorance can be forgiven. Hell, maybe we all deserve a second chance and it's been about fifteen years, so anyway, welcome to the club...friend."

"Thank you, Miss Hick," he said, shaking her hand, "for being so understanding."

Ms. Jarrett's clapping was joined by spectators in witness of their embrace. Mike grabbed the sleeve of Nard's shirt, unaware of his parents' new-found friendship.

"Would you look at yo' parents, playa'? Love is definitely in the air everywhere."

"Are my eyes actually witnessing this?"

"Yes you are, homeboy. The rekindling off a new beginning."

"Momms, yo' son ain't mad at'cha at all."

"I'm so glad you could make it, Meka. It's been a while, and no one had heard from you. Why you vanish like that?"

"I didn't. Your homegirl met someone that she could relate to better."

"Where is he?" She looked past her.

"He is a she. Her name is Diamond. That's why I'm here now…to let you know that ever since that night with us, my body only craves for the tenderness of a woman."

"To be honest with you, I only done it out of curiosity after hearing so much about how satisfying a woman can be when it comes to pleasing another. Unfortunately, that's not my preference. Strictly dickly for me."

"I see. Well, thank you for the invitation."

"You still my homegirl no matter what."

"Thanks. I think it's time for me to move along. Someone is waiting on me out in the car."

"Why you leave your company out there like that? You could've brought her in with you."

"Nah. She's alright. We 'bout to head out of town anyway."

"Meka, any time you need someone to talk to, or a friend to lean on, you know where I live."

"Thanks. And by the way, enjoy that midget of yours, girl."

"Oh, believe me, I will."

Meka's head rested on Shenequa's shoulder. She did the same, and struggled withholding her tears.

"Take care, Shenequa."

"You do the same, Meka."

She watched Meka exit through the door. Tosha walked up beside her.

"Was that that fool, Meka?"

"None other."

"Where she going? She ain't leaving yet, I know."

"She said she had somewhere else important to be."

"Important to be! You kiddin'! What she think this is? Child, let me go and catch this fool right quick."

"How you feelin' tonight, Mike?"

"Like a two dolla' ho'."

"Come on, man. It can't be that bad."

"Not yet, anyway."

184

"Maybe some of this punch drunk I'm mixing up will help you mellow out some."

Nard poured half a bottle of Bombay he brought into one of the punch bowls.

"Dad," a voice said from the dance floor, "po' me a lil' bit of that. I'm thirsty."

"Hook 'em up a small cup, Nard."

"My pleasure. Lil' man, there's a lot of young girls in here for you. See any you like?"

"Yeah. Over there by the speaker across the room," he said, taking hold of the cup.

"Why don't you run and introduce yo'self to one and see how she's doing?"

"How 'bout this, Unc'." He emptied his cup, sat it down, and pulled two roses out of a flower basket at the end of the table. "How 'bout I walk over there and get to know them both?"

He hid the flowers behind his back and made his move to where the girls were. Nard laughed at his nephew's brilliance.

"Now, Nard, you know betta' than to try my lil' twin like that. You'll be better off tryin' a grizzly bear cause my boy is always on point at all times."

"What you think about the scenery in here? It's lookin' lovely right now. Dime pieces everywhere. Who would've thought that temptation would begin so early right after tyin' the knot?"

"Twelve o'clock, playa'! Twelve o'clock! She's beamed in on us mighty hard, making a move in our direction."

"I see! I see! You ain't got to tell me twice!"

She eased between them, saying, "Congratulations, gentlemen." Her smile displayed sexiness. The fragrance she wore expressed desire. Nard's mind said yes. His heart pumped, "Hell no! Hell no! Hell no!" Mike felt an erection stirring in his pants. He squeezed it in hopes of the rushing blood settling. She fixed a plate at the table with little space separating her and Nard. A silverware dropped from her hand, and squatted at the knees to retrieve it. The warmth of her body pressed to his hind leg slithered upward. Intense passion escaped

185

through her thin, satin dress, reminding him of nights persuasion came easily for his chosen prey. He dared search the room, praying no one witnessed the minor incident. "And again, congratulations, Nard." His entire world left inside her swaying hips. Mike's hand waved back and forth in front of Nard's face, unnoticed. No longer did Mike have his friend for any company as he went to try and resolve some unfinished business.

"Umm, excuse me, miss, but don't I know you from somewhere?"

Mike continued guzzling extra cups of punch drunk in a fast motion, one after the other.

A PLAYA'S ENDING!

Printed in the United States
By Bookmasters